MW01223391

ALMOST PARADISE

Elizabeth Cain

iUniverse, Inc.
Bloomington

To Carol ~
May the gift of a
the horse add a
spiritual dimension to
to everything you do ~
Elizabeth Cain

ALMOST PARADISE

iUniverse books may be ordered through booksellers or by contacting:

iUniverse
1663 Liberty Drive
Bloomington, IN 47403
www.iuniverse.com
1-800-Authors (1-800-288-4677)

ALMOST PARADISE
Written by: Eric Carmen & Dean Pitchford
©1984 Sony/ATV Melody. All rights reserved by Sony/ATV Music Publishing LLC, 8 Music Sq. W, Nashville, TN 37203.
All Rights Reserved. Used By Permission.

ISBN: 978-1-4759-7353-2 (sc)
ISBN: 978-1-4759-7355-6 (hc)
ISBN: 978-1-4759-7354-9 (e)

Library of Congress Control Number: 2013901471

Printed in the United States of America

iUniverse rev. date: 6/21/2013

To Buck Brannaman, who taught me with patience and friendship the ultimate meaning of being with horses in the round pen and Charlotte Newton, who put the ultimate dance of dressage in my hands, also with patience and friendship. They are not in these pages as characters, but they were in my heart when I wrote the words.

PART ONE

1

When they led the horse into the round pen, I thought, *Okay, fifteen minutes.* It was a beautiful, dappled grey gelding coming along quite nicely with the handler.

"What's the problem?" I asked, taking the lead from his hand.

"Can't trim his back feet, much less get shoes on 'im. The farrier won't touch 'im."

"Where is he?"

"Over yonder."

"Tell him to get his stuff and stand by," I said confidently, already stroking the silver neck.

The cowboy left, shaking his head.

"Okay, pretty boy, let's see what we can do."

I circled a lariat around haphazardly, letting it brush him here and there, on his neck and back, against his chest. No reaction. He stood quietly. Some ranch hands wandered by the corral and climbed up on the rails. The sun was unbearable. I took the halter off the horse and stepped back. He pricked his ears. I turned and walked away. He followed me. I stopped and caressed him with the rope, on his face, over his ears. Some of the onlookers sniggered.

"Thatsa ways from his feet, lady."

I smiled. "It's a good thing the horse doesn't think like you."

That's when I noticed one of the guys who wasn't laughing. His face was framed by the top two railings, his hat pulled down shading half his face, but I didn't want to look away. He was just the most attractive man I had seen in a long time, and I wasn't that crazy about men. The greatest love of my life had been a horse trainer a couple of counties over—a woman. She said she loved me, but sexual stuff was off limits, so I guess I didn't really know what I liked. But that handsome stranger's eyes on me made a shiver go right through me.

The horse got in my space. I moved him back with the rope snaking in the air. No daydreaming for me. I saw the horseshoer had joined the group outside the round pen, pretending not to watch. He'd be in here soon enough with a hoof in his hand.

When I grazed the gelding's front legs with the rope, he stamped his feet. When I tried it with his back legs, he flat took off at a dead run! Round and round he went. He forgot I was even in there with him. I slapped the rope against my thigh, and one of his ears bent my way. I backed up. The horse slowed a bit and then stopped and looked at me.

"I think my fifteen minutes are up, boy," I whispered. "Come on. Let's give these cowboys something to talk about."

I haltered him and swung up on his back with the rope coiled in my hand. The horse relaxed. His reaction seemed to tell me *This is something I know.* I walked him around, petting him with the rope in the places he liked—neck, shoulders, rump. He got pretty comfortable with that. He was nice to ride, moved away from my leg, and halted with just a slight pressure from my seat. What on earth had they done to his feet?

He enjoyed being ridden. It was a reward to do this easy walk, trot, lope in the soft sand. The cowboys waited. A couple of women had shown up.

"You go, girl," one of them intoned as I went by.

I let the loop of the rope out over his head. We cantered. I had one hand on his mane and halter rope, the other on the loop. I let the loop bounce off his knees and brought him to a halt, leaving the rope right there. He didn't like it, but he stayed still. I removed the rope. He lowered his head a little. I slid the rope down onto his cannon bones. He leaped forward and almost unseated me, but I left the rope there and asked him to halt. When he did, I removed the rope. It didn't take long until I had the rope dangling on his hooves. He liked it so much just standing there quietly, understanding the halt cue and the release of the rope. We both heaved a sigh of relief, and a few spectators clapped grudgingly.

I didn't care about that. The good-looking guy had not taken his eyes off of me and now tipped his hat in my direction. I needed some water but couldn't stop for the sake of the horse. It was just about the hottest part of the day. The gelding was sweating but breathing easily, so I swung the rope around over his haunches and asked for the canter. Pretty soon, the rope was bumping his hocks. He kicked out a few times, but I kept cantering and letting the rope bump the places he resisted. When I asked him to stop, he slid into the footing and didn't move a muscle. I released the rope so fast I think it even surprised the horse.

We walked around directionless for a moment. Then I asked folks on the rail to pet him as we went by or just let him brush against their hands as I pushed him closer to them with my inside leg. The grey liked that too.

I turned back to the center of the ring, halted, and looped the rope over his hocks. He submitted. I flung it off and over his neck and let it fall to his feet. He turned his head and looked at me. *Is this all you want?* his expression implied. Then I went back to the hindquarters, letting the rope slip down below his hocks. He stamped his feet, left, then right. When both feet were still, just an instant in time, I pulled the rope back up onto his haunches. He stayed with me, that unshoeable thing.

I gently eased the lariat down the back of his legs until he would stand motionless, taking it away every time he accepted it. Finally I could pull the rope up from the ground, touching his feet, his fetlocks, his hocks and back to a coil in my hand. I leapt off his back and hugged him. "Good boy … good boy." I ran my hands down his legs lightly, first front, then back. I still had the lead-line, so if he moved, I could ask him to keep moving beyond his comfort level. When he stopped on his own, I put my hands on his legs again. At last I leaned against his left shoulder; his foot came right up into my hand. When I tried this at his haunches, he sidestepped away from me. I led him back to the center, picked up each front hoof, and then tried again with his hinds. I held his right hind until my back began aching, sliding one hand up and down between his hock and his hoof.

His head dropped down, and I swear he closed his eyes. No one on the rail spoke.

I nodded at the shoer. He walked in with his rasp and slapped the grey's rump. The horse startled, and I glared at the man.

"That's not necessary," I said.

"You gonna tell me how to do my job?" he asked sarcastically.

"No, I'm going to tell you how to help the horse and keep you from getting killed."

He ran his hand roughly down a back leg. The gelding flinched.

"Try making your hand feel like the rope," I said.

In a few minutes, he had the hoof in his hand and rasped it lightly. After all hooves were trimmed, he looked at me with a mixture of wonder and chagrin.

"Well, I guess this might work on other horses," he said.

"I guess it might," I said. "Now, how do you feel about rubbing him down and giving him some fresh water?"

"Not part of my job," he said.

"It is now," the great-looking guy on the fence said, and then to me, "Would you like a break?"

"That'd be fine," I answered.

There was a swath of shade on one side of the pen where a grandstand had been put up. I grabbed the rail when I reached it to keep from falling down. Someone's hands closed over mine, and a voice said, "Hang on. I'm coming in." The cowboy helped me to the ground and handed me some bottled water.

I opened my eyes to that wonderful face and said, "Who are you?"

He smiled. "I'm your boss."

"I guess I'd better get on my feet then."

"Oh, no, not yet," he admonished, pouring another bottle of water on a scarf he'd removed from his neck. Then he laid it on my forehead and sat down next to me.

"I didn't know I was hired," I said.

"You are definitely hired." He held out his hand. "Julian Rose."

I thought I might faint. He made me lean forward and put my head between my knees. His hand rested on my back. I felt like the horse, calmed and safe.

"Serena," he said, "I'm taking you to your cabin and ordering you some lunch. You look like the wind could blow you away."

"I get so interested in the horses, I forget to eat," I said softly. "What's next, anyway?"

"A trailering problem ... or should I say a *not trailering* problem."

"I've heard that before," I said.

"It'll be cooler later. I don't feel good about you doing it now."

He pressed the wet bandana against my head again. We were close enough to kiss. What a weird thought, must be the heat, so stifling, but my heart felt light, the woman I had loved not as compelling. Mr. Rose helped me up and kept his arm around me until we were at the door of a rustic cabin.

"I'll be back with some food. You all right now?"

"I think so."

"How 'bout some fruit and chicken salad?"

"That'll be great. Thank you, Mr. Rose."

"You're a hell of a horsewoman," he replied with a wry smile. "Where have you been all my life?"

"Trying to figure out who I am, needing horses to do it, and ..." I almost said *her* name.

Julian opened the door and said, "I hope you'll be comfortable here ... I'm likely to want you for a long time."

"Well, as long as I can help horses anyway."

"At least that."

He turned to go, but he must have known I hadn't gone inside yet, because he looked back.

"Serena," he said, "get some rest. I won't be long."

And the moment, whatever it was, was over.

I lay down on the feather bed. The room was cool, the windows shaded with thick, dark drapes, keeping the Nevada heat at bay. I could still feel Julian's arm around me. His strength, his sensuality flowed into me as nothing ever had before, except on the back of a horse. It brought tears to my eyes.

It was a beautiful ranch, cactus and juniper and gray-green

boulders strewn around, a turquoise sky, fields full of horses of every color behind pale oak fences, a soothing painting not quite real. My heart was racing. I ached for the next horse, for the next part of my job, for Julian's voice. I had applied on paper to be a *wrangler*, adding that I had an affinity with troubled horses. They could wonder why. I'd seen one photograph of the place—the wide log archway with black metal cutout of horses galloping across the top and a long, dusty road to distant barns and lodgings. It was far from *her*. It could be a refuge. I thought suddenly of Julian's hands on mine with the round pen rail between us. It might be the scariest place I could have found.

Just then Julian knocked, and I said, "Come in. I'm awake."

"Can't sleep?" he asked, setting a tray loaded with food on a small table near the bed.

"I'm thinking about the next horse."

"Not thinking about food?" He laughed.

"Can I think about the horse and eat at the same time?" I asked.

"I would say yes, but there is absolutely no room in there for me," he said, half teasing.

"And what would you like me to be thinking about you?"

"I just don't know yet. Maybe after the next horse, I'll have a better idea."

The next horse came soon enough. It was cooler, and a slight breeze had started up. Long shadows fell across the round pen from the thick aspens planted along one side, aspens Julian's mother had transplanted from a nearby spring-fed canyon and nursed on the drier ranch land with as much water as she could. Finally, her husband put in a drip-line from the well so the trees could live there forever around the rails after she could no longer care for them. One of the hands had told me this when I seemed surprised at the profusion of green on the border of the arena. But I turned my attention to the burgundy-splashed roan mare tossing her head and peering through the rails. Outside the pen, a truck was parked with a stock trailer hitched to it. It had a ramp but no dividers. It was spacious and clean.

Julian caught up with me and put his hand on my arm, kind of like I was one of the guys, which was all right with me.

"Listen, Serena, this horse has never been in a trailer. She's had her head in a vise and electric prods on her rump. She's thrown herself down and slid halfway under a two-horse. She's gone completely over backward with a lariat around her neck. I don't expect much. Do what you can, but stay safe. The fellows are going to give you a bad time."

"If the mare can take it, I guess I can too," I said, and I went in the round pen with two soft ropes.

"You wanta halter?" someone called out.

"Nope."

I began by playing with the ropes, just turning them and trailing them along the ground, ignoring the mare. I threw a few loops her way, but they landed shy of her. She ran a little but not in a frightened way. Her eye was always turned in toward me, no matter what I did. Did the boys know how much this meant? The mare was already including me in her world. Wow! I was really excited by this.

"Dumb mare," someone said.

I didn't hesitate. I said, "Mr. Rose, please take that man out of here."

"Hey, girlie, I work here too," he chided.

"But not with this horse. Not right now."

Julian sent him to clean and fill water troughs.

The roan could not contain her curiosity. Soft ropes were something she had never known, so I made her part of the game. I held out one large loop, and pretty soon she was mouthing it. I took it away and then made another loop. She thought she would try some other things, and finally she stuck her head through it. I did not tighten it down but flipped it off, moved to another part of the arena, and made a new loop. She found it and stuck her head in. The loops were different sizes, but I never closed one on her neck. Soon she was walking beside me with her head swiveling around inside that loop like it was the most fun she'd ever had. She knew and I knew she was testing it and learning to trust.

"That's the damnedest thing I've ever seen," someone said.

They just didn't know how good this mare was. They'd never

given her a chance to be good. I knew the trailer was not going to be easy, but I believed she would try.

"Can you guys back the trailer up to the pen and remove a section of rails?"

"Sure thing, Serena," one of them said.

Well, at least I was batting two horses and two cowboys.

While they were maneuvering the trailer, I increased the difficulty of the game, partly to keep her from noticing the object of her failure drawing near. I asked the mare to go with the loop, keeping her head in, wherever I moved—forward, backward, sideways, trot to halt, halt to trot. When she slipped out and ran off, I ignored her and kept doing figures with the ropes, tossing them against the fence and jumping into one of the loops myself.

She couldn't stand it and would come back for more. One time she pawed the ground a ways from me like *bring that thing over here!* I didn't budge. I watched her make the decision to seek that loop of rope. My arms got tired holding it. A stiff lariat would have been easier, but I wanted her to have a whole new experience that had nothing to do with the trailer and no reminders of what had happened to her in the past.

Everything was set. The open trailer fit in the space where there were no longer any rails. The roan and I played the game with her head in a big loop of lariat that I had never cinched down on her scarred neck. I went here and there in the round pen with her beside me, over to the trailer, backing away, going by the trailer right, going by the trailer left, sidestepping up to the opening. I stroked her and released her from the game from time to time. Then in one random moment when we passed by the open door, the mare's head loose inside the soft loop, I turned and walked into the trailer. And there she was, standing right with me. You could have heard a pin drop.

I handed the mare some hay from a net hanging inside the trailer, and then, with a motion of the soft loop, backed her right out, took the loop away, and sat down on the ground. She put her mouth on my hand where there was still the smell of oats. I thought, *Okay, girl, let's blow their minds,* and I put the loop up with her back to the open trailer. She put her head eagerly in the loop, and as I moved toward the opening, she backed herself right into the trailer. I was standing on the ramp. Her feet were completely in. She wasn't a large horse, and the trailer was extra wide, so I took a chance and walked up the ramp moving the loop to the right. She stayed with me and turned around inside the trailer, facing the front.

It was something I had never done. It was something the horse had never done. We had talked each other through it. When we backed out, there were fifteen ranch hands crowding around and praising that mare, just loving her and touching her gently. She just ate it up, forgiving them their former cruelty and frustration, as only a horse can do.

Julian came up and gathered me into his arms like a lost filly, which maybe I was. It felt good anyway, and I didn't want him to let go. Julian spoke over my head, "I'd like one of you who was never part of trying to load this horse to work with Serena and be this mare's only rider all summer, okay?"

A boy named Billy haltered the mare and took her to the barn, petting her neck the whole way.

"That was magic," Julian said.

"The horse was magic," I replied.

"I can't wait to see what you're going to do next," he said.

"Neither can I."

2

"See you at dinner," he called, releasing me suddenly and turning toward the barn, maybe a little embarrassed by hugging me with such affection.

Some of the other guys were slapping my back and saying, "Nice work." One pretty cute twenty-something cowboy squeezed my shoulder, but nothing felt like Julian's arms. I couldn't take my eyes off his lean figure in jeans and a white shirt retreating against a flaming orange sky. My insides felt like the fiery sundown.

Horses were nickering for their own dinner, pasture horses crowding the gate, and stall doors sliding open and closed. I shivered a little. The Nevada early spring evenings were cool, and I was especially tired. I walked slowly to my cabin. It was a Saturday night. The ranch tradition was for everyone to eat in the dining room of the main house, which I soon learned was Julian's, inherited from his mother and father who had developed the property years before but had died recently in a small plane crash. They had been searching the high country for more trail access for guests, searching at too low an altitude, and got caught in an afternoon downwind shearing off a ridge of sandstone cliffs.

"Mr. Rose says the highest off the ground he wants to be is on the back of a horse!" his foreman, Tyrone, told me. *That was the sadness in Julian's face,* I thought. He wasn't over it.

I looked disparagingly through my wardrobe. Jeans and more jeans, a nice pair of very snug black pants, English riding tights, lots of working tops, and one black dress. I was crazy about Native

American jewelry, so I could dress up almost anything. Most of my days were spent on horses, my nights in an oversized sweatshirt and maybe nothing else, depending on the weather, even with my dear Carla. Would she ever be laughing at my quandary over dressing for a *man*!

Finally I chose a clean pair of jeans and a gauzy white blouse. I would dress like Julian, but I added some old pawn turquoise and silver bracelets and a necklace of beads strung with three carved chalcedony horses. I didn't want to shock the cowboys too soon or make Mr. Rose think I was trying to impress him. I seemed to have impressed him just doing my job in the round pen. I didn't have time to wash my hair, so I pulled my long, ash-streaked blonde curls into a low ponytail, teasing out a few strands to soften my face. There was only a small mirror in the bathroom, so I didn't really know how I looked. I thought some blush and lipstick would give me some feminine appeal after my afternoon pasted in sweat and dirt. I grabbed a black jacket to match my best black boots and stepped out into the desert night.

The ranch house was alive with lights and music. Apparently their Saturday nights were cause for celebration. "Serena." A voice stirred the air around me. It was Julian. "I came over to get you. I wanted to make sure you were all right. You had a tough day." His voice was soft and, frankly, sensual coming out of the darkness.

"I'm okay, Mr. Rose," I said, hesitating to speak his first name, although I loved it. I had never known anyone named Julian, and I felt like savoring it privately, not squandering it in our first conversation. He didn't say anything else but took my arm gently, guiding me toward the bright scene. I wished that I could see his face. I wondered if he could feel my heart racing close to his hand.

He let go of me as he opened the door into the noisy dining room, but he turned slightly, and I saw an approving glint in his steel-gray eyes. "I like your Indian horses," he said, running a finger across their smooth stone shapes.

"My talisman," I said, meeting his gaze.

"Lucky for me too," he said, smiling.

The Mexican housekeeper had laid an inviting table, with colorful plates and bowls, and unbelievable fare created by Julian's Tanzanian cook, Askay. The woman, Marta, was tall and full-bodied, with a delicious smile and steady, generous eyes. The African was a slight man with a hearty voice, booming his welcome of me for all to hear. I relaxed.

Julian sat at the head of the table, and the rest of us scattered to find places. I ended up between Gayle, hired as a trail boss, and Joe, a seasoned wrangler adept at solving problems with horses and guests alike. There was no lack for conversation. I kept stealing glances at Julian's beautiful face. He still had on a white shirt, open at the collar, which showed off his deep tan. He and I were the only ones in white.

The food was remarkable, hints of spices from Askay's homeland, sweet onions and potatoes, and slowly cooked chicken wrapped in maize and crushed almond coating. The lettuce salad came last, with avocado, mangos, and a thin coconut dressing. We were encouraged to "eat up" because Curly, the barn chef who cooked for us all week, was partial to hamburgers and hash browns. This I learned from Gayle, who was a vegetarian and was given Askay's vegetables and Marta's salads any time she wished. A few of the boys didn't come Saturday nights. Carson, a Seventh Day Adventist, had church, and others had girlfriends in town about twenty-five miles from the ranch.

Soon Marta was clearing the table, and Tyrone and a couple of cowboys picked up guitars, softly tuned them, and asked for requests. We all mostly listened. Lara left early, so the three of us girls had ten guys to dance with. Julian gallantly led Marta to the floor, treating her like a member of his family, which I guess she was. Angie told me Julian's parents had brought her from Mexico, helped her become a citizen, and relied on her as their guest-ranch business grew. He didn't dance with anyone else, but around ten o'clock, he whispered something to Tyrone and came toward me, reaching for my hand.

The foreman had a lovely singing voice, and he began the heart-stirring phrases of "Almost Paradise." Julian did not hold me close at first, but he looked at me as the words filtered out into the room.

He touched my necklace again and said, "Here's a certain blue that matches your eyes." Near the end of the song, he pulled me right against his hard chest. I glanced around the room. Some were still dancing, enjoying the lilting melody, but Billy, the youngster who had been given the roan mare for the season, sat transfixed by our embrace. His eyes followed us as if trying to understand what he was seeing, trying to give it a name. Julian's hand moved down to my waist, and he pressed me even closer. My heart pounded against his. He didn't say a word.

Billy kept watching from a dim corner of the room, staring with unabashed intensity, and even though he couldn't know what he saw, I did. It was longing.

The next day was stormy and cold. A brisk wind came from the west, pushing dark clouds toward the ranch. Everyone tied rain gear to his saddle, and I noticed a few guys working the edge off their horses in the round pen. I was proud to see they were not just lunging, but giving the horses little jobs to do where they had to pay attention to the wranglers, earning some praise in the process. Julian was riding the grey on a loose rein in the larger arena. He seemed like part of the horse, sitting quietly and using subtle cues. *This is something he's been doing long before I came along,* I thought, and my throat tightened, watching him with feelings Carla had never aroused in me.

I'd been offered a buckskin gelding that had a habit of creeping up on the rump of the horse in front of him on the trail. My job was to break him of that habit before using him in the guest string. The first families were to arrive at the end of May, in about a month, and Tyrone had told us we had our work cut out for us. They'd gotten a late start shaping up the horses because of spring storms, still icy trails, and some messy bogs. The foreman detailed his plan for us as we started down the main road toward a drier patch of country.

Some of us would work in the arena, and some would make ten- to fifteen-mile trips into the Nevada wilds. The ranch sprawled over ten thousand acres, Mike told me as we headed south under the log arch with the words *Rancho Cielo Azul* burned into the wood. The sky was anything but blue that day. We'd guide folks over varied terrain, canyons and plateaus, and reach altitudes approaching nine thousand feet. Not too bad, unless you came from sea level. Those people would be taken on shorter rides and lower trails. But no matter where we went, the horses had to be ready and safe for inexperienced riders. A few guests would be good riders, and those horses needed to be tuned up to a higher degree.

I found myself beside Julian soon enough. He was describing his ideas for the ranch to Carson and a few others whose names I didn't know yet, so I listened in. He said his folks had wanted their guests to have the best possible experience, perhaps even more challenging than the usual riding adventure. The clients would herd cattle out of deep grass draws, check fence lines on rough ground, and learn how to be partners with their horses.

My mind wandered off. I was definitely distracted by the exquisite way he handled his horse, glued to the saddle and balanced like he was born there. I imagined myself on the grey with him, my arms around his narrow waist and my head against his back. *What on earth is wrong with me!* Suddenly he was saying, "That's why Serena was hired," nodding at me. "She has training in dressage, a mysterious concept for most of us, but I was thinking of adding some English-style mounts to our program. I have my eye on a black gelding over in California, but he might be too tall for most people, and he has big gaits." When he mentioned California, a dark look came into his eyes.

"I haven't committed to that trip yet," he said, and he added something, but the wind took the words out of his mouth and swept them across the sagebrush flats.

We trotted in silence then, and soon I went to the back of the line to work on the buckskin's attitude. We came to a steeper trail zigzagging up a red butte. The boys slowed to a walk, and in four strides, the buckskin was bumping the horse in front of me. He started tossing his head, expecting the usual jerking of his mouth, but I simply asked him to halt, counted three seconds, and dropped the reins. There was a nice space there for a few minutes, and then he was up on Joe's horse, a pinto mare who immediately took offense. I repeated the drill. It didn't take very long. Soon my gelding was *slowing down* as we approached the pinto, anticipating the easy halt and loose rein that followed. Joe looked back.

"Where'd you learn that?" he asked.

"It's just something I tried once and found that it works with most horses. If you have a horse it won't work with, give him another job until he learns it. Don't put a dude on him."

"Why not just sell him?"

"That would be up to Mr. Rose, but I think he's the kind of guy who gives second chances," I answered.

"You like him, don't you." It was more of a statement than a question.

I pretended that I hadn't heard.

"Well," he paused, "just so you know, he's very lonely."

Then things were taken out of my hands, or perhaps, put into them, in the least expected way.

We rounded a bend in a rocky switchback. Julian was a few horses ahead of me. The trail widened a bit, and on a high, flat rock, high as the saddle horn, lay a half-coiled rattlesnake trying to find some sun before the storm obliterated its warmth completely. Julian reached out with his rope to swipe the reptile off the cliff just as the rattler sank his fangs into Julian's thigh. I leaped off the buckskin and handed the reins to Joe, who looked on with horror. I yelled at Tyrone, who was just ahead of Julian, and he caught the grey's reins as I tossed them over the horse's head and got Julian to the ground.

Ty led the grey farther up the trail, after killing the diamondback, and I made Julian lie flat, reaching for the knife on his belt. I ripped his jeans open right where the snake had pierced them, cut an x in his flesh, and put my mouth on the wound. I sucked as hard as I could and then spit out the blood-laced poison, almost fainting with the effort and the vile taste. I knew there were better ways of handling a snakebite, but it was the fastest thing I could think of. Tyrone was holding Julian's and Mike's horses now as Mike bent down with a flask of whiskey.

"Serena!" he cried. "Rinse your mouth!" And then he poured some directly on the wound. Julian arched his back, breathing in painful gasps. He knew to keep as still as possible. And we all knew he needed something to counteract the poison. We were about four miles from the ranch. One of the women behind us on the butte shouted, "I've got the fastest horse! I'm going back for the truck. Can you get him down to the bottom?"

"Yeah! Go!" Tyrone urged, waving his hand at her. I hadn't realized there was a rider behind me—I had been concentrating so hard on the buckskin—but it was a good thing.

The men had to carry Julian about a half mile, taking turns leading horses or holding their boss steadily on the downhill climb. He did not once complain. By the time we reached the plain, we could see the truck flying toward us. I handed my horse to Joe and said, "I'm going with him."

The boys lifted him into the back seat. I bunched up my sweatshirt for a pillow and cradled his head. His leg was swelling now, and he was half-conscious. "Angie! Did you bring some ice?"

"Yeah, here," she said, tossing a plastic bag over the seat.

"Stay with me, Julian," I whispered. I figured that was the perfect time to say his name out loud. I set the ice gently on his thigh. He didn't react but moaned when we hit small berms crossing the desert. We turned onto the paved road, and Angie hit the accelerator. She had already called the hospital, and they were ready for him. We raced down the two-lane highway, barely slowing for the one crossroad that had a stop sign.

I hugged Julian to me, but he wasn't aware of it. He knew it was me, but he had no idea how I felt. I remembered fantasizing how, if Carla got hurt, I would hold her and comfort her, and she would love me back some way. This was an entirely new feeling, raw and powerful.

Once he opened his eyes and said, "Serena, I owe you."

"We're not there yet, cowboy."

He tried to smile.

We pulled into the ambulance bay. When they took him into the emergency room, they tried to keep me out. I could see he was scared, and I refused to leave him. As attendants poked and prodded him and shifted him roughly from gurney to bed, he grabbed my hand and squeezed it hard, seeming to say, *Please don't let me be sick in front of all these people.* I pressed my thumbs against a spot inside his wrists where the pressure sometimes relieves nausea. He whispered, "Thank you," and looked at me as if he recognized my heart from some far-off dream. Once he called my name, as his pain deepened, the drug not quite doing its job. I was afraid to let go of his hands, afraid that he would slip away from me, and I would never know the man behind the suffering.

A nurse came in and took his temperature, fussed with his pillows a bit, and then said to me, "You've been together a long time."

I stared at her. "I've known Mr. Rose exactly two days, ma'am."

"Love at first sight, huh?" she said.

I couldn't answer. I just wanted him to be okay. As soon as I was sure he was safe, the anti-venin, as the doctor had called it, dripping into his veins, I said softly, "Mr. Rose, I don't think this is in my job description."

He took a deep breath but could not speak just then. I don't know why, but I wanted to kiss him. I felt the same strange impulse I had when he pressed the cool cloth to my forehead in the round pen just yesterday. When he was able, he looked at me gratefully and said, so quietly I had to bend closer to hear, "They … couldn't kick you out, huh?"

"There was no way I was going to leave you in here alone. I'd climb right in that bed with you if it would help," I said, not knowing where *that* came from.

"Someday … when I feel better, I might just take you up on it," he said. He swallowed hard from some discomfort.

"Mr. Rose?"

"I remember you pulling me off my horse. I thought I was going to die, but my heart said, *Serena will know what to do.*"

"Apparently I made some mistakes …"

He put an arm around me and held me against his chest, whispering, "But *I* didn't. This time I didn't make a mistake," letting me wonder what that meant.

When he was mostly out of danger, I called the ranch. "Marta, Mr. Rose is recovering."

"Oh, gracias, Miss Serena!" she cried. "I tell everyone."

The doctor wanted him to stay a couple of nights, but Julian wouldn't hear of it, said he had too much to do with clients coming, horses to condition. A different nurse removed the drip, just saline now, and told me how to watch for infection. She couldn't have known I had only worked for Julian for two days and could never presume to stay in his house or his room, as much as I liked him. I felt I was already in over my head and needed to slow down.

Angie and I walked Mr. Rose to the truck. He had one arm around each of us.

"My two special girls," he said.

He was limping and said he felt dizzy, so we made him lie in the back seat, piling some blankets under him to keep his heart higher than the snakebite, another detail directed by the doctor. "And absolutely no ice!" the man had said. *We could have killed him,* I thought. At least I had known to keep him still on the way down the butte. He closed his eyes as Angie started driving, and I reached over from the front seat to touch his arm to make sure he was all right. He caught my hand and didn't seem to want to let go. I held it tight all the way back to the ranch, and it was so endearing. I thought of the time Carla grabbed my hand after a long road trip home from a horseshow and said, "I hate good-byes."

We left Julian at his front door with Marta and Askay, but he turned and studied my face. "There's more to you than meets the eye," he said.

3

In the middle of the night, someone was banging on my cabin door. I woke out of a confused dream about Carla, trying to figure out what she was saying to me.

"Miss Serena! Miss Serena!" Marta was calling.

I pulled on my jeans and opened the door.

"It's Mr. Julian! He ask me find you," she said quickly.

She took me into the ranch house where Julian was sitting in a corner of the living room sofa with his hurt leg on the coffee table.

"You should be lying down," I said.

"Can't," he replied.

"That's right … heart above the wound," I said.

"And no ice on leg," Marta added.

He was feverish but not dangerously so. "Have you had any aspirin?" I asked him.

"No … allergic."

Askay was pacing around behind him. I knew the Africans had remedies we had no name for, so I looked up at him. "Askay? Do you have medicine for fever?"

"Yes, miss."

"Marta, do you have mint leaves, ginger, and lime juice?"

"Yes. I can fix."

"Okay. Blend just small amounts with Askay's powders, Julian's antibiotics, and ice. Blend and add water until it's smooth and easy to drink."

"I'll go," she said, and they both hurried out, pleased to be able to help.

I was clutching at straws. I was no doctor, and I was ready to call him if my idea didn't work. I wiped some sweat out of my boss's eyes with the edge of my baggy nightshirt. I thought of how much better I looked in my black dress! Well, maybe someday he would see.

Marta leaned over and handed me the drink.

"I forgot to tell you *sugar*," I said. "It's probably bitter."

"I put," she said.

"Oh, thank you," I said to her, and then to Julian, "Drink some of this, Mr. Rose. Trust me." With a leap of faith, he took several swallows.

"I think I like this," he said. He drank more of the soothing liquid.

Not long after that, he fell into a fitful sleep. The room grew cold, and his chills intensified. Askay seemed to know what we needed, watching his beloved friend from the shadows of the room, and brought us a blanket.

"You stay with him, miss?" the African whispered.

"Absolutely," I answered, placing the comforter over Julian. Askay caught a corner of it, touching my hand gently as a prayer, and then left us. I held the covering against this almost stranger and felt his trembling inside my own body. Holding him closer seemed too personal, as some nightmare ate at him through the long hours.

As the light of day filled the room, he began mumbling. Suddenly he flung his arms, almost knocking me away from his side, and cried in a clear voice, "Miranda! No! No! Miranda, no!" and his fever broke. He startled awake and grabbed my shoulders.

"Serena! Were you here all night?"

"Most of it," I said.

"Oh, my dear, I'm so sorry."

"Mr. Rose, you needed help. Marta came and got me."

"Can't you say *Julian*?"

"Someday," I answered. He didn't know I'd already said it when he was half- conscious in my arms.

I got a couple of hours of sleep and then went to the barn. Some horses were saddled that I didn't recognize. "We just brought these guys in. They were on the winter range, didn't seem to care for the barn. We took hay and grain out to them, and they got pretty full of themselves. You up for some round pen work?" Tyrone said, all in one breath.

"Yeah, let's make some dude horses," I answered.

Before we even ran two or three into the pen, Julian was limping toward the small arena and climbing up on the bleachers.

"Mr. Rose, should you be out here?" Ty called.

"I think so. Let's see what you guys can do."

Tyrone turned to me and said, "How do you want to start, Serena?"

I was so pleased that he was willing to ask me for guidance. The other wranglers fell in line, asking questions and letting me show them new ways of relating to their horses. Julian encouraged them, and I praised them when they thought through a problem, especially when they used their own ideas to put pressure on the horse and then release. Some of the men and Angie were riding those *full of themselves* horses in the round pen with only a halter rope.

I helped one of the other gals, Lara, with an especially difficult big bay. He was snorting and prancing and hadn't even been caught yet, racing around the large arena, creating havoc with some of the animals just trying to do their jobs. We headed him off in a corner. I was on Julian's grey, and she on her favorite Morgan. As soon as the bay stopped and looked at us, we backed our horses away. He took a step forward. We backed away. When he tried to leave, we crowded him in again. Pretty soon he was traveling along between us. We delivered him to Alberto, who stroked him and spoke softly while the bay decided to put his head in the halter. "I'll take him today, Lara," Alberto offered, and she and I did a high five. Julian clapped. I waved to him and rode off to watch Billy work the roan mare, but my mind was filled with Julian's despairing cry, *Miranda! Miranda!*

We broke early for lunch. Julian stayed out in the yard as long as he could, gabbing with his boys and brushing a horse or two.

Whatever had happened to him, he was a strong man, standing up to his pain, both physical and emotional. We both had a secret that could shatter any relationship. I wondered who would tell first.

Later I eased two range horses into a dude horse frame of mind. Julian observed with the same admiring expression, but the effects of his nightmare lingered in his face. "Mr. Rose, you will not hurt my feelings if you'd rather be back in the house."

"I'm okay. You saving a horse is the best medicine a guy could have," he admitted.

"Does that mean I get a raise?" I teased.

"I'll look into that," he answered. He came down from the grandstand and met me at the gate, putting a hand over mine on the reins. No more words were necessary.

That evening, we gathered in the main house after our dinner in the cook shack (yes, hash browns and hamburgers) to discuss the upcoming clients. Julian asked me to sit next to him. I thought, *If he knew about Carla, he wouldn't be so interested in me.* I'd have to tell him soon. He trusted me. It felt like a lie, keeping the most intimate discovery about myself from him, that I had loved a woman. But right now he needed my horse savvy.

Mike asked right away, "Mr. Rose, if we get these horses so fine-tuned, how is anybody going to ride them? Conditioning them on the trail for the next thirty days is only going to make them stronger."

"Great question," Julian said. "Serena? Any answers?"

"My gut reaction is to give the clients lessons. Like with the buckskin. He's going to be climbing up the back of the horse ahead of him if the rider has no idea what to do," I said.

Joe raised his hand. He was the employee who had been with the Roses the longest. "What if we gave them a choice? Say we had some really sharp horses for folks who wanted lessons and give our older, rent-string horses to those who don't."

"Even some of those are getting pretty sensitive," Clint interjected.

"I agree about the lessons," Julian said. "We'll encourage

everyone to start in the round pen, maybe add an extra trail ride as incentive."

"Or maybe one of Askay's African meals," somebody quipped.

The laughter was good after the tension of the last couple of days. It was decided each wrangler would take four horses, learn their specialties and their weaknesses. Then when guests arrived, they would be directed to the cowboy that seemed to have the best match. After a brief trial period, I would take on horse and rider in the round pen, especially those needing or wanting extra help.

Julian said, "We've never done things to this extent before, just kind of prayed the horses stayed quiet all season. Now we're asking the horses to be their best and the guests to step up to the challenge."

Marta brought us all tea and Mexican cookies. For Julian, she had made the *fever cocktail,* as she began to call it, minus Askay's native drugs. "To the new season," Julian said, raising his glass.

"To Serena," Angie added, and all those hard cowboys echoed, "To Serena." But I think it was more for what I had done for Julian than for the horses, and I was okay with that.

The guys started out to finish evening chores. We had planned a ten-mile loop for the morning. There was tack to repair and clean, and a couple of horses had loose shoes. Julian caught my arm as I stood up.

Just his touch made me weak in the knees, but so had Carla's. Was this just a rebound crush? A crazy fantasy because Julian was so good to look at? I was half-afraid to find out, but I stayed. He wanted to show me the paintings his mom had done, mostly scenes around the ranch, luscious watercolors full of light and striking shades of golds and ambers, purples and blues. *Rancho Cielo Azul.* One picture had been turned around against the wall. It was in a dark corner, not very noticeable. I asked him about it.

"Those are the cliffs where the plane went down," he said with some emotion. "It was one of the first paintings she did. She loved that place."

"Tyrone told me about the accident. I am so sorry, Julian." I said his name easily in that moment and then added bravely, "If you turn it around, it will celebrate her life."

He brightened. "Of course. That's exactly what I should do."

He lifted the frame from its hook and let it face the room. It was a gorgeous place, red and pale yellow and rain-streaked gray cliffs rising from a wildflower-filled meadow into a cloudless, azure sky.

"Oh, Julian, I feel as if I know her, just by this one painting."

"She surely would have painted you, maybe on my grey, with the sunrise catching the waves in your gold hair," he said, putting his hand on the picture that had not seen the light of day for several months.

"My gray strands matching the grey, I suppose," I added.

"It would have been beautiful," he said, closing his eyes, as if trying to see it. "Funny how turning that painting around makes me feel, opening all of my mom's work to light. I'll have to think … about other things that way," he added, speaking more darkly.

I found the courage to say, "I have a picture turned around in my heart, against my heart right now."

"May I see?" he asked. I pulled out the locket I had just started wearing again facing backward, and he opened it and stared at the two figures, arm in arm, Carla and me.

"Serena," he said, "who is this?"

"My first love," I said with all the truth I knew.

"And you left her … to come here?"

"Lucky break, I guess. My life needed a different direction."

He encircled me in his arms and said, "I don't think I properly thanked you for saving *my* life." He closed the locket and kissed me with so much feeling, I didn't want him to stop. It was a kiss Carla had never given me, an embrace she had denied me over and over.

"I don't mean to scare you, Serena," Julian said when he finally moved his lips from mine. "It was just the best *thank you* I could think of."

"It was the best I've ever had," I said.

"Too soon … for us?" he questioned.

"Maybe, but please don't take it back," I said quickly.

"Your … friend. What's her name?"

"Carla," I whispered.

"Carla has a place with you," he said, touching the locket. "I'm trying to find my place with you."

"Well, keep trying. I need to know why kissing you is so damn wonderful."

He kissed me again. "Does that help?"

"No … pretty soon I won't be able to find any language to say what I feel."

"Me either," he said, releasing me like a cherished bronze he had held too long and was afraid to tarnish. "I guess I ought to thank that damn snake," he added with a smile.

4

But after that gracious kiss, we semed to get lost in our separate realities. My work with the troubled horses was exhausting. Julian got a good deal on a string from a ranch that was selling out, and they needed a lot of attention. He always found me at least once a day to applaud my diligence and ask if he could do anything for me. It was so sweet of him that I waited eagerly for the sight of my boss crossing the yard or climbing up on the rail.

Several of the new horses had *scratches*, sometimes called grease-heel, a terrible condition usually starting in the horse's heel, especially in the warm, wet seasons. The heels and pasterns could get galled, and then an opportunistic infection could travel higher up the leg, eat into the tendons, and lame a horse for life. I had not, to that date, discovered a reliable topical treatment for the crusty scabs, but I did know of two ways to deal with them. One involved a complicated medicated wrap, followed by deep cleansing of the area. It was difficult to scrub the heel first, because it could be extremely uncomfortable for the horse. The second measure, which could also be preventative, was to shave the hair from the affected part of the leg with electric clippers.

It was definitely a two-person job. I singled out the worst cases, and Julian helped me with most of them. Those horses had never *seen* clippers, much less been touched by them. Even the leg-wrapping was not easy, especially on the back legs, and scrubbing the scabs off with hot, soapy water was next to impossible. Julian was so patient with those animals and wouldn't let me do the hind legs if the horse even offered to kick. One time, his hand got badly bruised by an out-of-the-blue strike, and we both sat back against the stall wall trying to figure out how to handle the horse. The scratches had broken out high up on the cannon bone, and the horse was in real trouble. It was a lovely chocolate palomino with huge light dapples. His coat looked as if the sun had burst through holes in the barn roof, its rays splashing down on the gelding.

I sent Carson to the main house for some ice, and Julian let me hold it against his hand to keep the swelling down and relieve some of the pain.

"We could tranquilize him," I said, watching the horse stomp the leg we had been working on, "and maybe add some Bute."

"Let's give him the pain med and try again in the morning," Julian said. "I think we need a break. This just kills my back. How 'bout you?"

"My knees always start hurting after the fourth horse," I admitted.

"I guess we need the Bute too," he said, laughing and pulling me to my feet.

In about a week, we had most of the ten affected horses on the mend. "Remind me not to buy horses with white socks," Julian said, although a couple of dark-legged horses had the infection too. His hand was still swollen and sore, but he never mentioned it. That Saturday night, he had to rest his injured hand on my shoulder, because he couldn't close it around my hand for the last dance. Just briefly at the end, he moved it to my cheek and then let go.

On a late spring morning, we all chose our favorite horses. Then a few trades took place. Billy, of course, couldn't give up the roan mare per Julian's instructions, not that he would anyway, and Angie, for sure, wanted the half-Arab. I took Julian's grey until he was okay to ride (he had actually broken a bone in his hand), the buckskin, the big, rank bay nobody wanted, and one of the winter range horses, a sturdy, small pinto I thought I could use for a teenager. Each day, we'd ride one and pony one on the ten-mile loop. The next day, we'd work out the kinks in the round pen, and the following two days do the same with the other two horses. Julian would help as he could. He enjoyed watching me teach the grey his flying changes and spins, but he knew I missed my dressage routines.

One afternoon, we sat in the grandstand while Billy played with the roan. He was working up to trailering the mare short distances and had the rig backed up to the round pen. I'd ridden the buckskin ten miles that day, and the gelding had never forged up on the horse in front. Julian asked, "You know that big, black horse in California?"

"I remember," I said.

"I'm thinking of going over there after the first guests leave. Do you want to go with me?"

"Oh, Julian, are you sure? You don't have to buy a dressage horse for me."

"But I want the best for my Serena."

His Serena, oh God, I thought. He touched my neck and found the chain and locket gone. "I can't wear it here. It's not me anymore. And yes, I'll go to California with you."

He looked away for a moment. "There's another picture I have to turn around," he said softly. "It's been in a dark corner for fifteen years, and it's time for it to face the light." He paused. "I should do it by myself," he said, "but I don't think I can. After my folks died, I just couldn't handle conflict or mistakes or ..."

"Or what, Julian?"

"Meanness."

I said, "Julian, you don't have to tell me now. You have to heal and help me with the horses and ask me to dance Saturday night."

"Oh, I will definitely do that, my girl," he said with a bit more fervor.

"Serena! Mr. Rose!" Billy cried. He had the mare in the trailer.

"Okay, son," Julian said, "just take her out to the crossroads and back. That's far enough. And grab Mike or Alberto to go with you."

"Yes, sir, Mr. Rose."

"Well, if that doesn't beat all," Julian said. "I was dreading this season, because I just wasn't up to it. Now I'm relishing every moment—snakebite, broken hand, and all!"

We kept our eyes on the truck and trailer as it turned out the gate toward the crossroads. The sky was streaked with cobalt and orange and violet, the desert floor deepening gold and granite with pinpoints of pink from blooming cactus, the mountain a jagged charcoal.

"What was your mother's name?" I asked Julian.

"Helen."

I lifted my hand toward the coming twilight and said, "Just like one of Helen's watercolors."

The guests would begin to arrive a few days later, and we all realized our lives would not be our own. We had our wrangler Saturday night, everybody still working out problems and offering each other advice on particular horses and trails.

"There's still a bog down by the second loop creek crossing," Clint reminded us.

"Gayle's paint still tries to jump the ditches," Joe added.

All the animals had been bathed and clipped and polished, even the two rescued greyhounds, the ancient Border collie, who always trailed the first mile out and then wandered home, and a blue-eyed, red Siberian husky.

When the guitar melodies filled the room, Julian was still in a serious discussion with Andrew, one of the new hands who had taken offense at the dress code. A few guys were asking Lara and Gayle onto the floor. I went over and sat next to Billy. It seemed to surprise him, but soon he was telling me how his parents had left him at Mr. Rose's ranch for a *cowboy experience* when he was eleven and never came back. Julian tried to track them down, but they had left the country. Later, Julian learned there had been warrants out for their arrest; Billy didn't know why. He said, "Mr. Rose figured they had done the best thing for me. I graduated high school last year … only a B average, but Mr. Rose thought it was great. I love him like a dad anyway. And damn if I wasn't jealous of how you turned his head in the round pen! But then, you saved his life. So, Serena, I guess we can be friends."

"I guess so, Billy. I'd not take his affection from you, believe me," I said.

"You might not have a choice, miss."

"I … just left a relationship. I'm not looking to jump into anything."

He laughed. "Well, I'll tell the boys that. They're all wondering about you."

I had the last dance with Julian, the sound of "Almost Paradise" captivating us, and our holding on to each other captivating Billy. Even when Angie asked him to dance, he shook his head and kept his eyes on us. I felt wanted in such an erotic way that the dance itself felt like making love, even though I had no idea what that meant. I just knew it would be harder and harder to go back to my cabin alone, but Julian never stopped me.

The first couple was from New York. The woman rode English, and we had to disappoint her, but told her of our plans for the following season to have English tack and hunter-type horses. She was a good rider, so we gave her the big bay out of my string. Her husband knew nothing about horses and didn't want lessons. "Just give me any old thing," he said brusquely. "This was my wife's idea anyway." Tyrone had a quiet Quarter horse for him, so we didn't push the lesson idea.

The other couple was from Oregon and had been on a few trail rides, but they thought the round pen lessons would be a waste of time. The woman was small, so she got my pinto, and Joe had an older Appaloosa that was quite content going head to tail down the road. We all shook our heads and hoped for the best.

Julian said, "I guess if they're on vacation, lessons seem like too much work."

"What if we showed them what they were missing? Take one of their horses that maybe didn't behave so well on a trail ride and do a round pen demonstration," I suggested.

"That's a fine idea, Serena," Ty said, "but you'll have to be the one to do it. You already have enough responsibility. You'll wear yourself out before the summer is half over."

"Well, we have to start somewhere with the *be-a-better-rider* campaign. They'll tell their friends, and maybe the idea will catch on," I suggested.

It worked. After one afternoon when I rode the little pinto in figure eights with no hands on the reins, brought him to a sliding stop (the Oregon woman had had trouble stopping him), and backed up ten steps, and Billy demonstrated *trailer loading* after telling the guests the roan's grievous story, everyone but the apathetic husband from New York wanted lessons!

It was so rewarding for everyone, especially the horses, and Julian had clients for life, minus maybe the New Yorker, who thought the desert and the horses were boring. I thought of the day weeks ago when Julian had looked at me with interest through the round pen railing, because of what I was doing with his horses. It was definitely not boring.

That Saturday, the wranglers joined the two couples in the main house for dinner. They had been having their meals there with Julian while Curly reminded the rest of us how many ways hamburgers and potatoes could be cooked. The couples were leaving on Sunday, and we were all counting on some rest. The vet was coming Monday to treat a couple of lame horses, and the next group wouldn't arrive until Thursday. There would be a family from Washington with four kids and two sisters from Florida. Julian had already told me there wouldn't be time to make the trip to California that week.

The current guests were thanking Marta and Askay for the wonderful meals, and then the sound of guitars got everyone's attention. "This is a treat," the New York woman said, and we all danced, changing partners and cheering for the musicians, and then came the last dance. Julian took my hand from the arm of the Oregon husband. Billy sat in the corner below Helen's painting, and "Almost Paradise" floated out across the room. Julian put both arms around me. As we moved slowly by that corner I heard someone say to Billy, "I didn't know they were a couple," in an almost shocked voice.

Billy smiled, his face rapt with the vision of Julian and me, and said. "Oh, no, ma'am. They're just friends."

That night I could have done it. I could have made love to Julian. His body clasped to mine, his voice bringing the words to life in my ear, and his hands keeping me so close caused a burning to course through me like a flame. I didn't want the song to end. When the music died and the guests left for their cabins, he walked me out to the porch and said, before sending me off into the dark, "Serena … you'll never know what you have done for me."

Later, I lay in my bed thinking, *And what you've done for me is just the beginning.* I felt like a bronc in the round pen, not knowing who I was, what my job was, when the pressure would be released. Then I remembered when Julian said, "Hold on. I'm coming in." I fell asleep with those words in my head, dreaming of their ultimate meaning for my life.

5

The summer wore away. Julian started riding his grey, and I got a read on the big bay. Most of the guests raved about the lessons, even if they only got their horses hooked on to them in the round pen or cantered a few times in the fenced circle with their arms out in the air, their reins dropped on the saddle horn. It was exciting and demanding.

A few times, thunderstorms kept everyone inside. I tried to write some poetry, but the lines that had come so easily for Carla, *I have danced in the red snow/ where the spring has frozen/ where she finds me open/ I do not flee with my fresh wounds,* were locked in another reality and not so bitter when I thought of Julian. I remembered the day he let a nine-year-old girl ride behind him after her horse went lame, stumbling on a manzanita root and tossing the child to the ground. She cried, and her mother became hysterical.

He called to me, "Serena, could you ride with Mrs. Wahl, right up here behind me? I'll take Stella, and she'll be all right."

He actually sang to the girl, some old campfire song, and soon, she was chatting away about a rabbit she had seen that morning. He was telling her how they were going to take care of the horse that had fallen. Surely I could create that touching image with my pen. But no … just remembering that scene was poem enough for me.

One time he looked at me across a noon campfire, with guests and horses milling about, the wranglers packing away half-eaten lunches, and I saw tears at the edge of his eyes. But when I got up and went over to him, he said, "It's just the smoke, my girl."

The *my girl* took my breath away. It was something I wanted, but something I didn't understand. We both went back to our jobs, our miles in the saddle separated by wanta-be cowboys and kids that had to be watched constantly.

Saturday nights brought a pang of anticipation for the moment he would touch me and I could curl up in his arms for a few minutes. "My lovely Serena, how did you do this week?" he would ask.

"Horses were fine. Clients were happy. My heart is falling through a storm," I would answer.

"I know, sweet girl," he'd whisper, brushing my hair back from my face and almost kissing me.

"Almost Paradise" haunted us with its line, *We're knocking on heaven's door.* Where was the key? Sometimes he gave me a quick hug on the darkened front porch if there was no one around, but he never said *stay.*

One weekend in August, we had a cancellation. It was hot, and the horses were getting a little balky. We turned them all out in the hundred-acre grass pasture, and they raced around joyously until the heat brought their energy down a notch. Julian asked me if I felt like a short ride; he wanted to show me something. "Sure," I answered, grateful to be alone with him.

We saddled up and rode north a ways and then turned sharply off a familiar trail. After about three miles, we climbed into a treed canyon. Water tumbled down a small stream by an overgrown path. Julian pointed to where it burst forth higher up in the canyon. "It's from a spring," he said. "It's never been dry."

In another mile or so, the draw was filled with tall, healthy ponderosas, white pines, and lush aspens. The canyon narrowed, its walls towering above the trees, its sandstone faces sparkling with rough quartz. I wondered why we had never brought clients here; it was so beautiful. Then the cliffs boxed us in and held a surprise—a small house of squared timbers set at the end of the trail. It had a screened-in porch, a chimney for a fireplace, and lace curtains at the windows.

We dismounted, let the horses drink out of a large trough, which was filled continuously by a hose connected to the spring, and then tied them to an old hitching post under a ponderosa. Julian led me up the steps. One of the boards was broken. "Have to fix that," he said. He opened the door. It wasn't locked. It would be a hard place for just anyone to find. Inside were soft couches, Navajo rugs, many of Helen's paintings, and shelves of books. He opened the windows, and a cool breeze blew in off the creek. We were both silent for a minute, and then Julian said, "This was my folks' first home. I was born here."

"It's wonderful. I can see what kind of people they must have been. Look at all these books and your mother's watercolors! Julian, tell me about your father."

He wandered around touching things, things that were his dad's: a well-used rifle still in its rack on the mantle, a pair of silver spurs and some rusty ones piled on an end table, some books about stream preservation and humane fencing, and last year's calendar marked with appointments and town meetings.

"My father," Julian began. "He was a quiet man. But when he said something, it was important. Sometimes he didn't say enough. I remember my mom reminding him that my brother and I were too young to understand what he meant. One time, he showed us how to walk behind a horse. *Go right alongside touching the flank and stay real close all the way around.* My mom said, *Henry, tell them why.* Dad said, *The horse has got to know you're there, not be startled. If you're close, you just get pushed away. If you're two or three feet from that hoof, it's going to land a mighty blow,* and he expected he'd never have to tell us again."

Julian pressed his hand to one side of his head. "He used to get these headaches. I get them too. He'd be in his room a couple of days. My mom would tell us to go play in the barn. Sometimes Jason and I would only eat once that day. When we got older, we learned the signs and just went about the chores without him. It scared me so much. I thought he was going to die. One time when I was about sixteen, the doctor advised him to take some aspirin. He went into convulsions. It was horrible. It's why I don't take the stuff."

"You're not allergic?"

"No. I just can't get that picture out of my mind, my dad suffering like that. I've had maybe five headaches like my dad's, where I couldn't even talk, but I don't know if you can inherit such tendencies. Mine have come under extreme emotional distress, so I guess five is not such a bad number. The last one was after the plane crash. I felt blinded by the tiniest light. Marta hovered over me, prayed in Spanish, which was comforting somehow, and I got through it."

He paused for a moment, as if remembering that terrible day, and then said, "Some things are easier to deny than *get through*, you know? Then you walked into the round pen, and my heart took a breath for the first time in fifteen years."

My hand flew to my mouth.

"Of course, I didn't know about Carla. That could've put a kink in my plans." He smiled that wonderful, heart-wrenching smile.

"Well, it definitely put a kink in *my* plans," I said.

"Carla must be wondering if she made the right choice. If she's not, she didn't deserve you," Julian said more seriously.

I put my hand on a bronze statue of a horse pulling his rider out of a fire with his teeth on the man's lariat. I looked at Julian. "When were you here last?"

"Not since my folks died," he answered. "Askay takes care of the place for me. They spent a lot of time here after they built the new ranch house and I got old enough to run things. My brother had left home by then." He glanced around.

Was he seeing the ghosts of another time?

"It was their secret hideaway. I … I kind of had plans for it myself … but things didn't work out," he went on in a subdued voice.

"Can you tell me?"

"I was going to spend my honeymoon here. It's very special to me."

"Julian?" I had to ask then, or I never would. "Who's Miranda?"

He collapsed on one of the couches and drew me down next to him.

"My wife," he said.

"Oh, God."

"I'll tell you about her. I'll tell you everything." He seemed unable to look at me right then. "She's crazy, Serena. I haven't seen her in eight years. She means nothing to me now. I waited so long for her to get well. I've paid thousands for doctors and medications. She's devious and strong, a very dangerous combination in a schizophrenic. She killed two of my horses, and she tried to kill me. I got her committed to a facility in California, but even they have had a hard time handling her. I tried to divorce her, but the court says she isn't competent to sign the papers. That's the last time I saw her."

He stopped talking and leaned his head back against the sofa. I got up and poured him a cup of the sweet spring water we had filled our canteens with, and he went on, visibly shaken.

"There are some legal steps I could take to get the divorce without her consent, but when she finds out, she's going to *hurt* someone. You can't reason with her. God, you can't have a *conversation* with her. I let the years build up, my anger too, and she has no idea. She thinks I'm coming to get her, that we can go on with our married life, which lasted all of about three months. It just makes me sick."

All I did was rest my hand on his forehead, but tears sprang to his eyes.

"Don't say any more, Julian. Heaven knows I have my own pain, but I'll give you all the peace I know if it's just this brief touch. Please take it, Mr. Rose," I said, formal again. I was really a stranger to his troubled life. Sure, he liked me. He felt comfortable on Saturday nights in a crowd holding me close, but this, this intimacy, was perhaps not what we could handle yet.

"But, Serena, how did you know the name Miranda?"

"When you were having a nightmare after the snakebite, you cried her name. I was afraid to ask."

"Afraid is the key word," he said. "If she gets released, our lives will never be the same."

"I'm definitely going to California with you now," I said.

"Well, *that* is not in your job description, my girl," he said, smiling at last. "It's way riskier than the round pen."

"Maybe I'll learn something new, something I can use in the round pen."

"Hmmm. You are a delight, Serena Skye," he said. He lifted my hand from his head but kept a hold of it.

"Have you heard anything from the hospital or institution, wherever she is?" I asked.

"Just a few days ago. She's trying to get out. The doctors want me to come see her. I dread it so much."

"It will be a difficult thing, but I could meet her with you," I offered.

"No, Serena, you would definitely be a threat to her, and she's good at annihilating threats."

"What can hurt people who have each other's back?"

"Only Miranda, with her weapon of choice," he said bitterly.

Suddenly, a summer storm broke over the old house with sound and fury, and it signified everything ... everything that was to come.

We rushed out into the wind-driven rain. The horses were already shivering. We cantered as much as we could on the narrow, rocky trail. When we reached the flatter ground, the storm abated, and we collected the bay and the grey to a trot. Soon the ranch appeared under a huge rainbow. The boys were bringing some of the thinner-coated horses into the barn. The cabins and fences were freshly washed, their inconsistencies in the wood emerging as dark shadows. In all directions lay a scene for Helen's brush. I think Julian felt that too. Tyrone took our horses, and we headed for the main house.

Marta helped us out of our wet jackets and said she was making some of Askay's African tea. We sat at the kitchen table waiting for the soothing mango-flavored liquid. Julian lifted some hair out of my face and said, "Have you talked to Carla?"

"No. I don't know what to say."

"Won't she be worried about you?" he asked.

"Probably."

"Where'd you meet her, anyway?"

"At that big English riding school outside of Battle Mountain. She was my dressage instructor. We were all kind of out of sync with the popular scene, you know, cattle country and rodeos trying to define everything. Carla just let it slide right off her shoulders. She'd say, 'Girl, someday there'll be such a thing as *cowboy dressage!*' She was so sure of herself. I was a novice."

I told him then how she had singled me out, gave me extra time, showed me moves and tricks of the rein and leg with her hands on me, how that touch had changed my life, how I didn't think it meant anything to her at first.

"I found myself at the barn all the time, watching her ride or taking a lesson or going to horse shows. We were surrounded by people, but I only had eyes for her. She filled a place in me that had been empty, and I thought I could be that for her. It was a fantasy. I know she wanted my love, but only emotionally, not physically. I either had to push the sex thing or get out of there."

I paused for a bit. I didn't know how far I wanted to go with this. Julian was silent, just letting me be in that other time. But he put his arm around me and squeezed my shoulder.

I said, "*That* touch tells me I might have done the right thing."

"So, would you like to see her again?"

"I could see her now. The thought of it doesn't make my heart race anymore," I answered.

"We could invite her to a *Saturday night*? She could bring some girlfriends, uh, *straight*, preferably. The boys wouldn't mind new dance partners. Maybe she'd even help us find horses at some point, for English riders."

"She'd love that," I said. "She has a good eye."

"Well, she picked you," he said with a mischievous grin.

"It's more like I picked her. I had the harder time letting go anyway," I admitted.

He handed me the phone. I dialed the number slowly. "She's probably on a horse," I said. But she answered on the first ring. "Carla, it's me … I'm okay … I found a great job on a dude ranch, Rancho Cielo Azul … It's about two hours from you … I want you to come up here … no, really. The owner is thinking of offering English riding for his clients and buying me a dressage … I know, isn't that fantastic! … You'd have to spend the night, but here's the thing. We have a traditional Saturday night where everyone eats in the main house, and then we have live music and dancing … There're only four of us, five if you count the housekeeper, and ten or fifteen guys, depending on who stays around that night. They're pretty tired of the same old dance partners. I was hoping you could bring Lynn and Cheryl, maybe Alicia. We'd have dinner … and get caught up … No, it's casual, but sometimes we gals dress up, because we mostly live in jeans and T-shirts … You would? … I miss you too. Well, check with the girls and pick your Saturday. Our season is winding down, so there won't be too many guests to distract Mr. Rose and me from talking with you and the gang."

I repeated Julian's number and assured her she would be glad she came. We said *I love you* and *bye for now*. Julian smiled. "Won't you feel better reconnecting this way? Kind of turning the picture around?"

"I think it will be just what I need. You are an angel to do this."

"An angel or a fool," he suggested.

"Never a fool, Mr. Rose," I said.

We sipped the tea while the rain poured on the timbers of the house, almost drowning any more conversation. So much had already been said that words did not seem adequate to ease the deluge in our histories. Julian did caress my hand and say, "We'll talk later … about California." A beautiful new horse and a crazy wife. Would we be able to bear both? I thought about the possibility of Carla and Julian in the same room. *I'll wear the black dress. I'll show her a sea-change she's never seen before.*

But it didn't happen right away. Carla and two of the girls couldn't come for three weeks, and we had plenty of guests to deal with. The folks who had canceled rescheduled, and some friends of the Oregon couple wanted to be fit in before we closed for the winter. I spent hours in the round pen and on the trail. I learned every corner and expanse of the landscape. Marta and Askay prepared a couple of cabins for my friends, and Julian took a few wranglers out to fix fence and trail hazards. I started eating dinner with Julian and the guests in the main house but slept in my own bed every night.

I guess I should say I tried pretty hard not to fall in love with Julian Rose. Whatever was between us, I know for a long time we explained it away as missing the passion we once had, mine for Carla, and his for his wife before she became ill. We both had broken hearts and didn't really trust relationships, but somehow we felt safe with each other.

Two weeks before Carla came to the ranch, a gorgeous young woman showed up and hung on Julian like a queen bee to a hive. Her clothes were pricey and impeccable, and she fit nicely in them. She chose Julian's trail group every time and never came near the round pen. She hinted a lot about riding out alone with him, and boy, did I dread Saturday night. She was a good rider, and I watched, amazed at her nerve, side-passing her horse so close to Julian that their legs touched.

Then, in the middle of the week, at a campfire where everyone was roasting hot dogs and singing under the stars, she snuggled next to him on a log bench designed for two. He could hardly be rude to her and, in fact, maybe liked her attention, as far as I knew. But when he saw me at the edge of the fire ring, he excused himself and got up, saying, "Serena, I need to talk to you about something."

"Yes, sir, Mr. Rose," I said in my best employee voice, and walked off with him into the darkness. Before too long, he grabbed my hand and led me up into the grandstand.

"What do you think of her?" he asked rather seriously.

"Not *my* kind of woman," I answered.

"Nor mine," he said. "I think I've been spoiled by a little round pen wrangler."

"You always know the right thing to say."

"*That* gal might not think so," he said with a short laugh.

We stayed out there until we were both shivering, talking about the horses and ways we could improve the housing or the ranch events. Even the silences were comfortable, our shoulders barely touching in the darkness.

"Do you want to go back?" I asked.

"No … I'm right where I want to be," he said softly, never letting go of my hand.

Saturday night was a fitting end to that week, because I didn't just have the last dance with Julian, I had every dance. The young woman didn't have enough nerve to cut in. She was dressed to make any guy take a second look, but Julian didn't even look once. Near the end of the evening, he said, "You make me feel alive again. I absolutely could not stand to touch anyone else right now … but, Serena, please don't let me smother you."

I just said, "I can go a long time like this without oxygen."

When I went back to my cabin, I saw the woman waiting in the shadows of the ranch house. I turned, in spite of my vow not to care quite so much, and there was Askay in the doorway, politely saying, "Main house closed now." And that was that.

Among the next arrivals were five guests who had known Helen and Henry Rose, and they had come specifically to ride to the cliffs. Julian had not been there since the accident. I had never been there, so I was surprised one morning when Ty handed me Julian's grey and my big bay, tacked up and ready to go, and said, "You're riding with Mr. Rose today." We usually split up, or else Julian was on the trail and I was in the round pen. Today we would escort only the five who were friends of the Roses to the place where the plane went down.

These people had been coming every season for ten years, three couples from Colorado. One woman's husband had died in the last year, but the other couples had encouraged her to keep their tradition of August at Rancho Cielo Azul. It couldn't have been a prettier day, a truly azure sky with a few wispy mare's tail clouds floating across the horizon. The desert was drier now and not as colorful, but some recent afternoon thunderstorms had dampened the trail and cooled the air.

No one said much riding out. There were the Barclays, the Sloans, and Ruth Helms, the widow. They were probably in their sixties, the same age as Julian's parents, and competent riders. Julian led, and I followed last but found myself next to Ruth, who seemed to want to engage me in conversation. She asked about the round pen, how the horses changed in that setting, and how the guests took to lessons. I answered as completely as I could, but I could not keep from worrying about how hard this ride was going to be for Julian.

Ruth was saying, "You're quite fond of Mr. Rose, aren't you?"

"He's been very good to me."

"Helen and Henry's son … a very special man. I don't know you or anything about your life, so forgive my presumption. He needs someone who has her feet on the ground and her head on straight."

I had to smile at that unintended pun, *straight*. Feet on the ground I could do, maybe. I said, "Ma'am, I'm as down to earth as they come." And I told her about the rattlesnake and how I demanded to stay in the emergency room with Julian.

She said, "You'll do just fine, young lady!" And we cantered along to catch up with the main party.

The cliffs loomed out of the wide expanse of sagebrush and scattered cactus. The sandstone walls rose up almost one thousand feet above the desert floor, and from a distance, in the shimmering summer light, mirrored the watercolor image Helen had painted many years before.

Julian slowed the pace down now, perhaps reluctant to finally be in that place, or maybe because a good trail had not really been established yet.

"Do you folks want to stop here awhile?" Julian asked.

Everyone seemed to want to say his own good-bye to Julian's parents. Some continued circling on horseback. Others dismounted and knelt on the rough ground. I reached Julian, who was still sitting on his horse in what must have been the exact spot where the Roses lost their lives. He rested one hand on the cantle of my saddle, and I leaned against him.

"Thank you for bringing me here, Julian. I know this is not easy," I said.

"I seem to need you here. I seem to need your strength, your steadiness."

"It hasn't been my best quality lately, except maybe in the round pen," I said.

"And here we are in *this* round pen where neither you nor I nor God could save them," he replied in a choked whisper.

"But now you have this beautiful new trail loop, which is what they were looking for. It gives them life somehow, don't you think?" I asked.

"It does, Serena. I wouldn't have thought of it like that, but it's true," he said and smiled for the first time that day.

The Roses' friends were all on their horses now and telling Julian they were ready to go, thanking him for sharing that place with them and assuring him they would still be coming every August, as long as they could climb on a horse. On the way back, Julian and I rode side by side.

Then a few days before Carla was to come, Julian got a phone call from the facility where Miranda had spent the last fifteen years. She wanted to see him, claimed she was *well* and sorry for *the way things ended*. She was on her meds and asking to be released. Julian's face paled as he told me this.

"Serena, I just don't believe it. She is beyond help. I'm convinced of it."

"What will you do?"

"You and I'll go to California after Carla's visit, which is *this* Saturday, I guess. We'll drive with the horse trailer, so we can pick up the black if you like him. I'll talk with the lawyer that knows the case. Miranda will never give her consent for a divorce, but maybe the lawyer will know a way out of this mess. I shouldn't drag you into it. Not much frightens me in this world, but that woman scares the hell out of me. She should be locked up and the key thrown away, as the saying goes."

"Maybe that's too harsh, Julian. People do get well."

"She can fake getting well, but she'll never *be* well," he said. "It's a catch-22. I could help her get released, if she'd divorce me, but then she'd be loose. Everything I love would be in grave danger. I can't take that chance."

He called the institution and agreed to see Miranda at the end of the month. The only thing that brought joy back into his face was inquiring about the black gelding and making arrangements for me to ride him.

"I know nothing about dressage," he said.

"Some of the moves you cowboys do could translate nicely into the shape of dressage. I think you'd really enjoy it," I told him.

"Give me an example," he said.

"You know when you're doing a side-pass or a forward leg-yield, let's say to the right, keeping the horse straight?"

"Yeah."

"Now picture bending the horse's head and neck to the right as you go, making sure the legs are crossing laterally in that direction and maintaining the forward momentum. That's a half-pass. Your grey already does that. I just haven't shown you yet!"

"You can do dressage in a western saddle?"

"You can, but I think the horse feels your leg and seat a little better in an English saddle."

"That makes sense," he said, "but how 'bout the bit?"

"A snaffle is best. The western curb can't give you or the horse the right feel. And a hand on each rein gives the rider more ways to shape the horse."

"Isn't that like *plow-reining*?" he asked.

"No. There's more finesse to it than that. You can actually define a right circle with your horse with a *left* rein!"

"Wow. That I have to feel. But aren't the gaits different?"

"The gaits are the same, basically. There's nothing artificial about dressage, but there are extensions and collections, rhythms and flexibilities that suit breeds other than cowboy horses. Do you know what the black horse is?"

"Not for sure," he said. "All I know is he came from Europe, some kind of warmblood."

"I can't wait to see him!" I exclaimed.

"You'll be riding the black horse of your future while I'm dealing with the black monster of my past. Ironic, don't you think?"

"It's very sad, Julian. For both of you."

6

The morning Carla, Cheryl, and Alicia were to arrive presented the unique Nevada fall day. Cumulus clouds puffed up into an ocean-blue sky. The breeze had an inviting warmth to it, and the aspens bent in graceful shapes around the arena. The smells of Askay's African dishes being prepared made my mouth water. But I was nervous. It felt like the peaks of many waves on a restless sea were coming together on the dry, white sand.

I got on Julian's grey and practiced some half-passes and canter pirouettes, which the horse could do, cantering with all four feet in motion in a tight circle, although he could do a stock horse spin just as readily. Julian had gone to town for a haircut and something new to wear for our Saturday night. I couldn't imagine anything sexier than his blue jeans and white shirt, sleeves rolled up and open at the neck. I thought of my black dress and high heels I was going to wear to surprise everyone. Would it be too much?

I was just then executing a perfect half-pass when Carla's truck turned up the driveway. It stopped once. The girls were taking pictures. Then they pulled up to the arena and came to the rail.

"Wow!" Carla exclaimed. "You can't take the dressage out of the cowgirl!"

"Hi, guys," I said.

"Whose horse is that?" Cheryl asked. She gave us both an admiring look.

"My boss's. Mr. Rose."

"And he approves of dressage?" Alicia asked with an air of disbelief.

"He approves of *me*, and that's who I am," I answered. I dismounted and ducked under the rail to hug them. Joe had come over, and he took Julian's horse for me after greeting my friends.

Carla hugged me the way she always had. She didn't hold anything back. Neither did I. It felt good, but it was in no way as *complete* as the feel of Julian's arms. I would always love Carla, but I would never want her the way I wanted Julian. It was a defining moment, but sad too. It was like giving up a piece of myself that I never really understood but was so sure of.

The girls asked to see everything, so I took them into the barn. The farrier was shoeing horses, and some of the boys were stacking hay and replacing stall boards. I introduced them to the three and then pointed out my favorite horses and explained what I had done with them in the round pen.

"Where's Mr. Rose?" Carla asked.

"He had to go to town. He'll be back for lunch."

"Something sure smells good," Alicia noted.

"That's dinner. Pure African," I informed her proudly.

"Really?" she continued.

"The best food you'll ever eat, guaranteed," I said. "Of course, we only get that on Saturday night," I conceded.

Billy drove in with the roan in the trailer. He'd taken her with another horse on a longer trip. I told Carla about how that was one of the first horses I had had success with. We wandered toward the house, just as Julian returned. My heart skipped a beat. He got out of the truck and came over and kissed my cheek, and then he put his arms around Carla. I guess he recognized her from the photo in my locket.

She laughed. "Well, I don't know whether to be more surprised at you kissing Serena or you hugging me!"

"Both things feel quite natural to me," he responded with his beautiful smile.

Carla turned to me as he spoke to Cheryl and Alicia. "There's a guy who knows how to hug!"

"You got that right," I said.

"Are you …" she started to ask.

"We're very close," I told her.

"He seems like a true gentleman, and so handsome."

"I'm afraid he sort of pulled my heartstrings on the first day," I said.

"And that's just what you needed, Serena," she said, giving me a little hug.

We all went in to have the lunch that Marta had fixed since Askay was working on dinner. Soon Carla was in a huddle with Marta, contentedly conversing in Spanish. Carla's father had been a native from Mexico, supervising a large crew on a bean ranch on the coast of Southern California when he met her mother, who was teaching English to the workers' children. She and Jorge had had a wild and secret courtship. Her parents were still together, running a hotel in La Paz.

While we ate, all the talk was about horses. Afterward, Carla noticed Helen's paintings and made a big fuss over them, which pleased Julian. He showed her which scenes were places we took guests on trail rides, and she remarked that among those images there was country she'd like to see. "That's quite possible," Julian said. "You'll have to bring your own tack." That led to the discussion about English riding lessons for clients and maybe even dressage clinics. Would she be interested in doing that? She agreed it might be fun but told Julian she had seen what I had done with his grey and was certain all he needed was me. *More truth than she knew to that,* I thought.

Julian said, "Well, it's a ways off. I'd have to rewrite my brochures, buy more horses, and attempt to appeal to dressage riders who want a *Wild West* vacation. How many of those people are around?" We all laughed. Nobody could imagine the answer to that.

Tyrone came in and took the girls out to their cabins. I put my head on Julian's chest.

"You okay?" he asked.

"I'm so okay," I answered.

"Nice gals," he said.

"My best friends. Thank you for caring about them."

"Not hard to do," he said and gave me a quick hug. "I need to make some phone calls. Shall we see each other again at dinner? You can spend some time with Carla and the others."

"Sure … until dinner then?"

"Can you come over a bit early? I want to give you something," he said mysteriously.

"I'll be here … about five?"

"That'd be fine," he said.

I spent the afternoon in Carla's cabin with Alicia and Cheryl. They were ready to apply for a job! They were single and attracted to the lean, sun-tanned wranglers they had seen riding or working in the barn.

"Well, you'll get to dance with them tonight," I said. "A few of them have girlfriends they're bringing out. It's our end-of-season special Saturday night."

"We brought riding clothes and something dressy. What's best?" Cheryl asked.

"I'd go dressy tonight. I've been wearing jeans all summer, but tonight I'm wearing a black dress … for Julian."

"Serena, what is it with this guy?" Alicia asked.

"We really get along well. I mean … he's more than my boss. He's very dear to me. I can't imagine a life without him in it," I answered.

"Sounds like love to me," Cheryl said. "What's holding you back?"

Only Carla understood part of that answer, because, unless I was as obvious as stars in the night sky, no one knew about the two of us.

"Isn't he a little older?" Carla wanted to know.

"About ten years," I said, "but at this point, it doesn't seem to matter."

"Is he married?" Cheryl asked.

That one rocked me. "It's complicated," is all I said.

We parted to get ready for dinner, and I had to hurry to be back at the main house by five o'clock. I showered and slipped into the black dress, a lovely creation of ruffled short sleeves and looping folds of silk from the bodice down. The neckline was low but appropriate. I stepped into spiky black heels and rolled my hair up in a loose knot. They say women dress for other women, but I knew that this dress that I had saved all summer was definitely for Julian. But I guess I wouldn't mind if Carla had a little twinge of *something* when she saw me. I walked carefully to the ranch house to keep from spraining an ankle. Joe rode by and whistled. "Do I know you?" he said.

Julian greeted me at the door and looked stunned. "You are a vision," he said, "and I have just the thing to make it complete. Come with me." And he led me into his bedroom, where I had never been. It was spacious and filled with books, Helen's watercolors, bronze horses, and a quilt he said Marta had made him that complemented all the colors in the room and in his mother's paintings.

"I love this room," I said.

"I have imagined you being here from time to time," he said. "Close your eyes."

I did and felt him put something in my hand.

"Okay … open."

I looked down at the small necklace. On a silver chain hung a pendant, a black diamond surrounded by a heart of white diamonds. The diamonds caught the light of the setting sun flickering through the filmy curtains on the windows.

"Julian … this is the most beautiful thing I have ever seen."

"My dad had given it to my mom the day they crashed. It was retrieved out of the wreckage," he said in a barely audible voice.

"Oh, Julian, how can I ever wear this?"

"I want you to have it," he said.

"I'm honored. I truly am."

"So am I."

He fastened it around my neck. "My new talisman," I said, touching the gorgeous stone and then tears that had fallen from Julian's eyes.

"The boys know the story. Billy is the one who brought it to me. You can tell your girlfriends, if you wish."

"I think I'll keep it to myself," I said. I wondered how Billy ever discovered this on that devastated site.

A few of the guys were arriving, and I could hear Carla introducing herself to Mike and Alberto. Julian sent me out so he could change his clothes. I felt exposed somehow, wearing Helen's necklace and holding Julian's secrets deep inside. This was beginning to be the largest crowd we'd had, in spite of what I had told the girls. Marta and Askay were bustling around finding extra chairs and table settings. No one spoke to me for a moment, and then Carla came over and said, "You are a vision."

"That's what Julian said," I told her.

"Well, we've got good taste," she said brightly. She fingered the necklace. "Did he just give you this?"

"Yes."

"Serena, he seems too good to be true," she said.

"He's true all right, but he's dealing with something … unsettling. I know he's lonely, but he hasn't been with anyone for fifteen years. I don't know if the one he's waiting for is me."

"I'm on your side, girl," she said.

Just then Julian came out of his room. He had on black jeans and a mostly white shirt with thin vertical lines of black about six inches apart. He was wearing new black boots and a black silk scarf, but the shirt was unbuttoned like I liked, although he didn't know that then, and I swallowed hard. Not just because he *looked* good, but because he *was* good. He took my hand and Carla's and seated us on either side of him at the long table filling up with wranglers, clients, and my friends. Julian seemed to be holding Carla in esteem because she loved me, and it was one of those surreal moments that happen in life, moments you can hang on to when other things are falling apart, other choices are eating at your soul.

The camaraderie, the food, the music—all were unparalleled that particular night in late September. But the highlight, of course, for me, was the last dance. Julian had danced with each of my friends in turn. He told me later that Carla had said to him *Take care of her*, and he had told her that's what he lived to do. I took a spin with Alberto and Joe, who kissed me on the cheek and led me to Julian when the first strains of "Almost Paradise" drifted across the room.

For the first time, no one moved. Julian and I were the only ones dancing, in a tight embrace that seemed to stun the crowd to silence. Tears rolled down Billy's face. Did they see that we were on the edge of some as yet undeclared dream? They could not have known about our commitment to confront the terror in Julian's life or face the unknown in mine.

Julian whispered some of the words. *I thought that dreams belonged to other men, 'cuz each time I got close, they'd fall apart again … It seems like perfect love's so hard to find … Almost paradise.*

7

There was that song again, sweeping into the cab of Julian's truck as we sped down Interstate 80 toward California. Another talisman, but then that word *almost*, enough to make us stop the truck and cling to each other. The last call from the institution informed us that Miranda screamed that if her husband didn't come get her out, she was going to strangle someone. They didn't believe her. Julian did.

"Julian, let me drive. You need a break," I offered.

"No … thanks, Serena. It helps to have something to do," he said. He swung back into the fast lane and then to the truck lane, remembering the horse trailer.

I knew he wanted to face Miranda with the truth, that their life together was over, that he wanted a divorce, no matter what she said or how she had calmed herself down to appear normal.

"Even if her meds are working," he said, "how could I sleep in the same bed with her?"

"Julian, I wish I knew the right thing to say. Mental illness is so inexplicable. No matter how you define it, the person just doesn't fit in the real world. That's not to say *normal* people always fit either."

A few miles passed while the sounds of "Almost Paradise" reminded us of days on the ranch, cantering under a blue sky, dancing as if there was no one in the room. I said I wanted to be with him at the institution, that I couldn't stand for him to go alone.

"Serena, if Miranda knew about you, there'd be no hope for her recovery or your safety. I shouldn't even have brought you, but you need to see the black horse."

"Are you going to leave me at the farm?" I asked.

"The manager said there was a guest room. You'd be safer ... and able to ride the gelding to your heart's content. By the way, you'll never guess what his name is ... *Cielo Negro*."

"*Black Sky* ... fitting," I said with a sigh.

"The mental facility is about an hour from the farm. It should only take a couple of days to figure this thing out. I'm already feeling like one of those headaches is lurking somewhere."

I rubbed his shoulders, and he seemed to relax. The lights of the first big city, Winnemucca, winked in the distance. Julian slowed down and reached up to squeeze my hand. "Tonight we'll stay together ... but no dancing," he teased. I knew what he meant.

I was very afraid for him. It would be so easy to say the wrong thing to Miranda. Her triggers may have changed over the years, her appearance, her deceits. It would be like approaching an IED. Innocent looking, and then *boom*. I was excited about the black warmblood but knew I would be beyond consolation if something happened to Julian.

Later that night in the motel room, we slept in the same bed but didn't touch each other. It was so comforting, just being close to such a beautiful and honorable man. I would not have known what to do. Although we had kissed a couple of times around the time of the snakebite, those were unusual days and seemed far from our present circumstances. Julian would divorce Miranda and start over in another arena. I had the black diamond on my neck. I wept for Helen, the woman I never knew, and for her son, who had changed the course of my life. I wept for the lost moments with Carla, when I had been so filled with desire and certainty.

The next day, Julian let me drive on toward California. He was fighting that headache, maybe more emotional than physical, but stressful nonetheless. I gave him some of Askay's remedies that I always had with me, and after a while, he said he felt better. He put his hand on my neck under my ponytail for a moment and said, "Boy, am I glad I hired you."

The miles passed. We tried to find "Almost Paradise" on the

radio, but no station played it. We were headed to the Sacramento Valley, another three hours on the road. I thought I could make it, but after we crossed the border, Julian said he'd better drive. The traffic was nerve-wracking after our quiet desert distances between towns. We stopped for a quick hamburger about noon, and I said, "I'll never complain about Curly's hamburgers again!"

Julian put his down. "These are pretty bad," he said, "but I can't eat much anyway." We shared some sweet potato fries but thought of all the delectable varieties of Askay's sweet potatoes and didn't finish those either.

"I guess we're spoiled—Nevada blue skies and African cooking," Julian said.

"And no congestion," I added.

With that, we climbed in the truck and in a while were driving down the poplar-lined lane into Serenity Farms. Julian backed the horse trailer into a row of trailers and started unhitching it. He wanted to leave from there, not see Cielo Negro until after I had ridden him so he wouldn't influence my decision, and so he could deal with Miranda as soon as possible.

We stood in the parking area, and Julian put his arms around me. "Thank you for being here," he said. "I'll call you as soon as I know anything. I have the guest house number," he told me, getting back in the truck.

"Okay," I said and reached for one of his hands through the open window, putting it on Helen's black diamond. "For strength," I added. And soon he was disappearing around a bend in the lane.

I felt as if the sun had left the sky. How could I ride in this sudden darkness of spirit, this weight of Julian's fifteen years with a woman who claimed his body and soul and yet could kill him? But I could think no further of these things, because there was the black horse coming out of the barn, tacked up and ready to go. He nickered at me, as if he knew me. I was smitten. And then I mounted and rode into a new world. *Cielo Negro*, symbolic of the black diamond on my neck, began to show me a different color, and in fifteen minutes, I had changed his name. *Cielo Bailando.* Dancing Sky. Because that's what he did, danced his way around the arena on the lightest aids. I was reminded of the first time I danced with Julian, how lightly he held me while communicating the deepest possibilities of our relationship. I couldn't wait to tell him how wonderful the horse was.

But when he called me that night, he was so distraught we didn't even speak of the gelding. "Serena …" his breath caught. "It was awful. She was skin and bones. She'd been starving herself until I actually showed up. Then she ate furiously with her hands. I could barely keep my lunch down. She grabbed my hands with her hands covered with food and begged me to *get her out!* I said I wanted a divorce. She flipped out, started throwing chairs at me and clawing at my shirt. I've already thrown it away. I don't think I can go back."

"Julian, the worse she behaves, the longer they'll keep her locked up."

"The doctors said, *No, try agreeing with her and see what happens.* So I went in again and told her I was sorry. I wouldn't divorce her. I'd help her get released, lying through my teeth, of course. She calmed down immediately. Well, yeah! But that's not going to happen. I told the doctors I was getting a divorce, with or without her. They said they'd up her meds and for me to come back tomorrow. Oh, God."

Then he explained how the facility was releasing patients that had been there over fifteen years and still had a living family member or guardian. He reminded them that she had tried to kill him, there was no way she could be released in his custody. But he agreed to return tomorrow. "Not before I see a lawyer," he added. "I'm not going to play tricks, bribe her, or lie to her. She and I have no future. If she can't accept that, she'll have to live with it. I just let her ramble on with her nonsense and swallowed more of Askay's remedies. I think I can sleep now."

"Julian, get some rest. I'll be anxious to hear about tomorrow," I said.

"My dear Serena," he said, and we hung up with many questions unanswered.

8

I was cantering in the half-pass and asked for a flying change when I got to the rail. It was effortless and smooth, so unlike what Julian was going through. I halted and dropped the reins, letting the horse relax and walk free. I thought back on the long summer, the hot trail rides with cranky guests, Julian supporting my decisions in those situations, the meals under the stars, Julian sitting down beside me and letting his shoulder brush against mine, the connecting with horses in the round pen and handing Julian the reins of a broke horse with such pleasure, dancing with Julian on Saturday nights, treasuring his breath on my face, his words in my ears. And I felt suddenly adrift without him, looking for a sign on the horizon to guide me to the place I was meant to be. I saw only Julian catching my eyes through the railings of his arena, his gentleness and respect drawing me into his life in such unexpected and wonderful ways. *Oh God, do I love him?* I thought.

Just then someone came into the indoor arena and motioned me over. "A trainer from Idaho wants to ride him," the man said.

"He's already sold," I said.

"I haven't seen any money," he said curtly.

"Mr. Rose is taking care of some business. I'm sure I can make some arrangements later today," I assured him.

"Well, I'll let the trainer ride but give you a chance to make the deal first, if you're sure."

"I'm very sure," I said.

When Julian called, I let him tell me about Miranda first. The lawyer had said he could divorce her on the grounds of undue stress and irreconcilable differences, even if she was competent on meds to consent or not. Her threatening behavior and her killing of the horses was on the record, and that alone could show *just cause* for a divorce. Julian felt more relieved, but Miranda was a zombie. He tried to reason with her, saying he had moved on with his life. She reacted to that, shouting wildly *No, no, no, no, no!* before lapsing into a catatonic state.

"I'll proceed without her, Serena. I don't even have to see her again. The bad thing is they could still release her if she finds somebody to take her in. It's not likely, but it will be a shadow over our shoulders. I made the doctors promise to inform me if she got out."

"The whole thing scares me to death, but I think you've done everything you can," I told him.

"Serena, what about the horse?"

"Oh, he's unbelievable," I said. "But another trainer showed up and wants him. We have to decide today."

"Do you want him?"

"I do … but it's a lot of money, Julian."

"I'll come to the farm right now."

I couldn't speak.

"You deserve it, Serena," he said.

"And what can I give you besides your now fourth-level Quarter horse?"

"I think you know the answer to that!" I could see his smile.

We were really headed toward dancing to end all dancing, and I was glad.

I watched for Julian while grooming the black horse. The trainer from Idaho had left him sweaty with a sore on his mouth. This was very unusual. Most dressage trainers were fanatic about cleanliness and the health of the horse. I wondered why she wanted him if she had to use so much leg and hand on him. Cielo Bailando rubbed his head on my shoulders, his dark eyes trying to gauge my intentions. "You'll have the best home ever," I promised him, and I thought of the big pasture and comfortable barn and lessons with Carla. Now I could concentrate on what Carla was teaching me, instead of anticipating her touch. When I thought of Carla now, I felt good. When I thought of Julian, I felt elated.

And there was Julian walking into the barn. He'd come in the back way, where he'd left the trailer. I ran into his arms. He held me tight. There was nothing to say. The farm manager came down to collect the check and suggest we wait until morning. Julian could stay in the guest house with me, if that was appropriate. "It's quite appropriate," Julian said, and the man went off to get Cielo's papers and a copy of his recent vet check.

Julian stroked the dark neck and said to the horse, "You are a beautiful thing, aren't you?" Cielo nodded his head. "I'd like to go tonight, but it wouldn't be fair to him, and we might need more paperwork for transport. We'll probably need stabling for tomorrow night, in case we aren't making it in a decent time."

The manager handed us a stack of papers. "You can see he has a negative Coggins," the man said. "All you have to do is have the vet call for the trip permit number. I think he opens at nine. Good luck." Not even a pat *good-bye* for the superb horse.

We went to dinner at Red Lobster. It was noisy, and we weren't very hungry. Julian called the ranch and told Tyrone to prepare a double stall for Cielo. He didn't say anything about his other business in California.

"We'll have to tell everyone about Miranda," Julian said. "We're all in danger, even the horses. I tried to get a restraining order, but you can't restrain a person who's already locked up. And I can't keep her out of Nevada, if she is released. When she finds out I've left, all hell will break loose."

"She'll have to find you," I said.

"Oh, she's an expert at that," he said.

"She'll never find your folks' cabin."

"You're right. That's what we'll do. We'll go there if we get the chance. The boys can say I'm out of town buying horses if she gets as far as the ranch. It'll be all right, Serena. It has to be," he said, pushing his shrimp around on his plate.

We both ate very little, anxious to be on the road, out of California, away from Miranda. Later, we lay in the same bed, and I don't know about Julian, but I was afraid of my sexual feelings. Did I want him because he was so devastated by his insane wife and half-sick with despair? Did I want to heal him or make him crazy for *me* as I had longed for Carla to be?

But Julian, of course, made everything right. "I could take away your soul tonight, Serena," he said, "but I think there will be a better time for us." And then, in the dark, he whispered the words of "Almost Paradise."

We didn't load the black until noon. Julian wanted to meet with the lawyer. I went along, and the lawyer seemed surprised. "If you two are having sex, it weakens your case," he said pointedly.

"We're not," Julian said, "but we care a lot for each other. It could be easily misinterpreted."

"Just be careful," the man said. "Things can get turned around in a hurry. I'm going to ask the institution to keep Miranda until after your divorce is finalized. Then you can get a restraining order for the date she'll be released. I know they're pushing people out after fifteen years, if at all possible, so we'll have to play our cards just right."

We left the office, went by the vet's to pick up the health certificate with the trip number on it, loaded Cielo, and were on our way to Nevada, glad to turn our backs on crowded towns and one deranged woman. I thought of Jane Eyre's Edward Rochester, locking his mad wife in the attic. Would we have to resort to such measures to have any relief from the specter of Miranda? Grace Poole still burned Rochester's house down. The parallel was chilling.

Then another thought came to me. Julian's wife had rights too, even if she became his ex-wife. Her illness was not her fault. But how could potential victims stay safe? How does a human stay safe around an angry or abused horse? I would dwell on these questions all the way home. *Home.* How easily that word came to me after one summer that felt like a lifetime. Was there a line in that song that fit all these emotions?

I'd almost given up. You must've read my mind. And all these dreams I saved … They're finally comin' true. I'll share them all with you …

We didn't sleep much. At four in the morning, Julian's cell phone rang. It was one of Miranda's doctors. The manic woman had tried to hang herself with her bed sheets when she learned her husband had left town. "He will pay, he will pay," she kept saying over and over, and then later, under sedation, she swore she loved Julian and would never hurt him. The doctor told him they had tried a new medication and believed Miranda could be released into someone's care.

"That someone will not be me!" he said firmly. After that, he paced the room, saying he had a pain in his chest.

"Julian, don't make yourself sick over this," I said, beginning to worry about him.

"Let's go get your horse. I need to be home."

So in the dark we loaded Dancing Sky and put more miles between us and Miranda's rage. The closer we got to the ranch, the easier Julian breathed. I decided he had not gotten over what was done to his horses all those years ago or the way she had tried to kill him. I wouldn't pry those details out of his heart. Some wounds take more than love to heal.

The sun was setting in a blaze of color through purple clouds. The desert was fresh and clean, like a painting. *Helen,* I said to myself, *I will protect your son with my life.* We slowed under the sign, *Rancho Cielo Azul.* It was a refuge, dependable and serene. Marta and Askay came running out, and then a few of the boys who had finished their dinner. Angie was beside herself to see the horse. Tyrone helped unload Cielo and led him to his stall, mumbling admiring words to him. Julian told Ty to bring everyone in the house after breakfast the next morning. *He is really going to tell them,* I thought.

Askay had a small supper prepared for us, and we ate it gratefully. Marta had figured out how to make the fever cocktail into ice cream, so that was our special treat. She didn't know how much we needed those particular ingredients. That night, and from then on, I slept in Julian's bed. He had nightmares, and he would let me hold him curled up behind him, but sex was the farthest thing from his mind. Maybe that wasn't entirely true, but he respected my innocence, the uncertain place that I came from, maybe some uncertainty that *he* was what I really wanted.

We had one more group of guests in the fall, and I got to show off the black horse. Carla came out a couple of times and worked with us and talked with Julian about the English mounts. We didn't tell her about Miranda.

But Julian had told all the ranch hands the morning after we returned from California. They sat in shocked silence around the big dining table, where we had had so many cheerful Saturday nights. Julian did not dwell on the details, just made everyone aware of the danger should his wife be released. He asked them to be thinking of a plan if Miranda showed up on the ranch and said that he and I would try to get to the cabin in the canyon.

"I think maybe she could get lost in this big ol' desert," Clint suggested.

"I don't want to hurt her, just keep her from hurting us or the animals."

"Why would she hurt the horses?" Alberto asked.

"Because she's done it before," Julian said and left it at that.

"Not while I'm watching out for them," Tyrone assured us.

"Serena will be staying in the ranch house so I can protect her. There's nothing to gossip about." Julian said this quietly, as if no other explanation was necessary.

"Mr. Rose," Billy said, "we are not going to let *anything* come between you and Miss Serena."

"That means a lot to us, Billy, but understand this—you guys are not safe either. If you get in her way, she'll strike like that damn rattlesnake. And she doesn't coil first or sound a warning. Trust me," Julian pleaded.

"Maybe we should start locking the main gate and the barn at night," Ty suggested.

"Gates and locks mean nothing to her," Julian said. He paused to settle his heart. "She burned up two of my best horses in the horse trailer behind a locked gate at a rodeo grounds in California."

Then, I believe, they finally got it.

"Mr. Rose?" It was Hugh, one of the newer employees. "Why did you ever marry that woman?" It was impertinent of him, but Julian didn't seem to mind.

"I didn't know she was ill. She was good around the horses but jealous of them almost from the beginning, of me spending so much time with them. She started saying weird things like *Why didn't you marry one of them* and *You'll be sorry if you don't choose me*. I just really didn't listen. She'd set small fires in the house and then say it was an accident, or she didn't like that chair anyway. By the time I tried to get her some help, she had tried to kill me. Look, guys, it was over fifteen years ago. I can't dredge it all up. I just thought if you knew the basic facts, you'd know how to deal with the situation. If any of you want a reference for another ranch, I'll be glad to let you out of your contract with me."

"I don't think anyone's leaving," Ty asserted, glancing around the table.

"If I hear anything from my lawyer or Miranda's doctors, I'll let you know," Julian said and asked them to go back to work.

In November, with the temperatures dropping and snow on the high ridges, Julian received the legal papers granting him a divorce. He put them in a drawer and came out to the barn where I was blanketing Cielo. He took my hands from the cold buckles and blew his warm breath on my skin. "It's over," he said, and then added, "except it's probably not really over."

"What can I do, dear Julian?" I said, wanting to erase the pain from his eyes.

He pressed my head against his chest. His heart was beating so hard.

"Marry me," he said in a hoarse whisper.

I was so startled, I couldn't answer right away.

"Or think about it," he said, framing my face with his hands

"I don't have to think about it, Julian. I'll definitely marry you."

Then I got the kiss of my life. It said so much. It said *I love you, I cherish you, I want you, I live for you.* Now I could not sleep in his bed. We were more than friends looking for comfort, a boss and his favorite wrangler looking for pleasure. We were going to be a holy union, and we would do everything right.

Then he put a ring on my finger. It was a white diamond surrounded by a heart of black diamonds, a smaller contrasting version of Helen's necklace. He must have started having it made right after we came back from California.

"Do you want to set a date?" he asked.

"You do it," I answered, still overwhelmed by the suddenness, the exquisite ring.

"Christmas day," he said. "Marta always makes a big fuss over Christmas. We might as well take advantage of her cakes and decorations. Askay could add some African traditions. And I just need you to be my wife. I need that more than anything."

"It will be the best Christmas I've ever had."

We embraced again in the dim light of the barn, winter closing in, the cold fact of Miranda in the shadows. But it wouldn't be so lonely in the darkness from now on, for Julian or for me.

10

It was a glorious winter, almost paradise, burnt-red bluffs blanketed in white, crisp mornings giving way to a bleak but welcome sun that kept the Christmas cactus blooming in the window and warmed our backs as we rode out checking the cattle and the range horses. The barn was filled with the scent of horses munching oats, the quieting scene of ranch dogs and cats curled in the straw, sometimes together, forgetting their summer spats, and the less rushed comings and goings of cowboys doing winter chores. The silence was healing, the snow on the windswept flats a shield against the truths of bare ground, bare hearts.

Many of the wranglers had city jobs in the winter, so with a skeleton crew, we all ate in the main house. Tyrone still played our song on Saturday nights. He and Alberto sang it as a duet now. Billy still followed us with his eyes with a hunger to know what we were feeling. Angie was the only gal still on the job, so she and Marta tried to give all the boys a turn. Julian felt thin in my arms. *Damn that woman*, I thought, trying to caress the hope back into him that we would be all right, in spite of Miranda.

We sent out personal invitations to our wedding ceremony, but most friends were involved with their families on that day, and that was all right. Carla would be there, Angie and the boys who stayed the winter. Julian's brother might come down from Montana. I had been emancipated at thirteen from my parents, and even though I had an idea where they were, I didn't think they would make the drive. They were good people, but the first time I asked for a horse and they said *no,* I left home and never looked back. I was selfish and headstrong, I realized now, but that was one of those choices that elicit loss.

One clear day near the first of December, Julian said he had an errand to run, so I spent some time with Cielo. I did some trot and canter down the wide, matted barn aisle, a few flying changes, and very short half-passes. It was just too cold outside, and the arena footing was frozen solid. Maybe I could talk Julian into an indoor arena next year, especially for the new English-riding clients. The black was enjoying the attention, but when I saw Julian pull in, I left Cielo and went back to the house.

He laid a brown-paper wrapped package on the kitchen table and sat down wearily. "It's tough getting to the cabin these days. I had to hike through the snow the last mile. I still want to go there on our wedding night."

"Me too," I said. I couldn't imagine being any place else.

"I found this where I thought I might, in my mom's keepsakes," he said, resting his hand on the bundle. "It's for you, but don't open it now. I've never seen it. It's her wedding dress."

"Oh, Julian."

"Will you wear it? She was about your size."

"I'll be grateful, truly," I said.

"Try it on. Marta can make some adjustments if you need to."

I took the package into the bedroom and laid it on Julian's bed, not rushing to open it. Helen's wedding dress. I had no doubt it would suit me, even though it wasn't the latest style. I carefully peeled back the brown paper. I stared at the lace and pearls set in the bodice ending in a thin stand-up collar. I lifted it out, breathless. The lace fell partway in a soft fold. Under that was floor-length satin, flaring slightly at the bottom, creamy white. It had long sleeves of lace, a thicker ruffle at the wrist, and little pearl buttons down the back. I undid them carefully and then straightened out long streamers of pearls dropping from the waist.

I loved it. I stripped off my jeans and wool sweater and eased the dress over my shoulders, letting it fall to the floor with a soft rustle. I felt transformed. A virgin in white, thirty years old, waiting for the moment that would reveal who I was. But no matter the answer, I would be Julian's wife. And if it was *almost paradise,* that would be enough. I hung the dress in the guestroom where I went, reluctantly, every night (Julian wouldn't see it there) and returned to the kitchen. Julian looked up expectantly.

"It was definitely worth the trip to the cabin!" I exclaimed.

"It's all right?"

"It's perfect."

"As you are," he said with light in his eyes.

"I guess you don't know that yet, do you?" I teased.

"I think I do."

We had a scare later in the day when one of Miranda's doctors called. Julian pressed the speaker button. Dr. Djandi informed Julian that Miranda had found a cousin willing to take her, and a release date was set for March. "Your wife insists she will be reuniting with you," the man said.

"She is no longer my wife, sir, but I appreciate the call," Julian said, his face draining of color.

"March," Julian repeated. "We can have our wedding in peace."

"Thank God," I said.

Marta was saying her own prayers.

Two days before Christmas, we rode up to the little house in the canyon. We'd had a Chinook wind, so the trail was clear of snow. We packed an extra horse with supplies for about a week and unloaded everything happily in the thirty-degree day. Julian replenished the woodpile and checked the chimney.

We ate a small lunch Askay had sent: African banana-rice-cucumber-mint salad chilled by the ride in, smoked chicken, and Marta's homemade honey-wheat bread. We felt blessed.

Julian said, "Remind me to bring that book, *The Art of Dressage*, back with us."

"Do you think we'll be doing much reading?" I said, hooking his waist with one arm.

He grinned.

We made up the bed with fresh white sheets, pillow cases with satin bands Marta had sewn on, and a winter quilt of ivory heart-shapes stuffed with down. There was a white down blanket in Helen's hope chest, worn but clean.

"Are you nervous?" Julian asked me.

"Not one bit," I said.

"May I have this dance?" He held out his arms, and I stepped into them. He half sang and half spoke the words to me, the words that had become so much a part of our lives since that first Saturday night. *I feared my heart would beat in secrecy. I faced the nights alone. Oh, how could I have known, that all my life I only needed you … Almost paradise. We're knocking on heaven's door … And in your arms salvation's not so far away. We're getting closer, closer every day … Almost paradise.*

The early twilight descended, and we did not want to let go, just moving to the music in our hearts.

"We'd better get home," Julian said. "Wind is coming up."

"Yeah. A cold one this time."

"Askay said he'd come up and get the fire going Christmas morning."

"Wonderful," I said, going out the door. The horses were beginning to fret in the sharp breeze.

We trotted a bit but felt even colder, so we walked the horses, gloved hand in gloved hand, across the flat plain patched with snow and stalwart cacti, and finally under the arch at Rancho Cielo Azul. There was a UPS truck in the driveway.

"More wedding presents, Mr. Rose," the driver said as we passed by.

"Thanks, Raol," Julian said.

"I got some of Marta's Mexican cookies! She always gives me something," he said as he swung into the truck.

"She's the best," Julian replied.

11

On Christmas Eve, we all went to St. Mary's Cathedral in town. Most of us weren't Catholic, but we seemed to want a special blessing that night. The justice of the peace was going to marry us. This would be our pledge to the divine. The nativity scene on the snow-flecked lawn was lit with white lights. Anthems poured out into the evening air as folks opened the wide doors. It was warm inside.

We left our coats in the anteroom and went down the aisle with our friends. The service commenced, and we took part in what we understood. At the end, there was Communion. People filed out of their seats, Marta and Askay, Joe and Angie. The priest beckoned to us.

"We're not Catholic," Julian explained, "but we're getting married tomorrow."

"Come, my children," he said. And he gave us the body and the blood of Christ, against his Church tradition. Then he added, "Peace and grace be with you in your new life."

It's something we would surely need in the coming months.

Julian parted from me at Angie's cabin with a feverish kiss and went to the main house. Helen's dress, my shoes and jewelry, and a new veil Marta had made to match the gown were in the wrangler's cabin. I wouldn't see Julian until eleven o'clock the next morning.

I couldn't sleep. Every breath brought me closer to Julian, to his pain, and to his joy. Where else did I want to be? I thought of Carla. I couldn't help it. I thought of the time we galloped through a mountain meadow, the grass as high as our stirrups, our horses plunging through the deep green, our legs touching as we slowed to the trot just before the narrow end of the field and the trail home. She had reached over and kissed me as we slowed even more for the first precarious curve in the abandoned track. It was nice. I had wanted it, but it was nothing like Julian's. Julian's kisses swept like fire through my whole being, with no questions, no reservations. But I was grateful I had loved Carla. It had opened my soul.

Angie whispered from her bunk, "Serena?"

"I'm awake," I said.

"Are you a virgin?"

"You got it," I answered.

"Are you scared?"

"No … maybe of any other man, but not of Julian."

"I'm so happy for you two. I remember the first day you came to the ranch. I was the one who said, *You go, girl*. I don't suppose I meant *after Julian!*" She laughed.

"I think I loved him the first time he touched me, but I really didn't know what that kind of love was."

"You had never loved anyone before?"

"Yes … but she wouldn't have sex."

"Oh my God, Serena!"

"I'm not gay, Angie. I just happened to fall in love with a woman. It's hard to explain."

"But if you haven't had sex with Julian, how do you know?" she asked.

"I just know," I said. "Like I know now it's not so much about the sex, but deeper connections and desires. I've thought about this a lot since Miranda turned up in our lives. If the woman I loved had had a crazy husband, I would have run like hell, not put my life on the line to save her, sex or no."

"That makes sense," Angie agreed. "If something happened to Julian, heaven forbid, and he couldn't have sex, you'd still love him with all your heart, love him more than you'd love any woman."

"That's right. I think you're explaining it better than I did!" I told her.

"Well, I hope it's everything you want. He's a great guy. I've worked for him for ten years. He's never looked at me the way he looked at you that day in the round pen."

Oh, if Helen could have painted that moment! I thought, but said to Angie, "Yeah … that kind of turned my world around."

"But you guys waited to sleep together. Because of that crazy woman. I can't believe it!" she said.

"She was his wife. He hasn't slept with anyone for fifteen years."

"Oh my God."

"Angie, I shouldn't be telling you these things."

"I don't gossip."

"I've noticed," I said, "but Julian is so private. I wouldn't want him to think I was betraying a confidence."

"I won't repeat a word," she promised.

"Thanks."

"Try to sleep, Serena."

"Okay."

But sleep never came, and suddenly it was Saturday, December 25, and I had three hours to get ready. Marta came over to help, but I sent her back to the house. I knew she had a million things to do, being an addict to *finishing touches*. Angie braided my hair in one long piece that reached the first of the satin ropes of pearls that fell from the waist of Helen's dress. I used some makeup to give some glow to my winter-white skin and a light peach lipstick. Angie made me use a little charcoal eye shadow and darken my eyebrows. At ten thirty, I put on the dress and low satin heels I'd found at the Native American thrift store.

Cars had been coming down the driveway for an hour. I wondered who was here. But I knew I would only have eyes for Julian. The justice of the peace arrived, and Askay was at my door. He would be giving me away, and Angie would be my maid of honor. She had picked her own dress, something she could wear again. It was the blue of the Nevada summer sky. Askay put a bouquet of flowers he had grown in his greenhouse in my hands—an artistic mixture of blue desert bells, white larkspur, gardenias, pale-blue and white columbines, deep blue violets, miniature white roses, and one black rose to match my necklace and the black diamond heart on my ring. It was his wedding gift, and he bowed as he gave it to me, saying, "These flowers of paradise, except for black rose. It is tie to earth."

It had started snowing, so Askay drove me the short distance to the main house. I waited with him in the living room while latecomers were seated. "Is Mr. Rose okay?" I asked him.

"He very anxious to see you. Very restless last night. We talk many hours."

"Thank you, Askay," I said.

Then Alberto began playing "Almost Paradise" on his guitar, and I walked down the aisle created in the long dining room with a white carpet someone had rented, I don't know who. When Julian saw me in his mother's dress, I thought he would faint. Tyrone, his best man, steadied him, and I moved slowly toward him. Some guests had been given rose petals of many colors to represent our Nevada sunrises and sunsets, and they threw them on the carpet in front of me. One of them caught in my hair, and as I reached Julian, he brushed it away and said, "Such loveliness I have never seen." I handed my bouquet to Angie and took Julian's hands. He had on a black tux, but the white satin shirt was open at the collar, and I just choked up.

The justice spoke briefly about the sanctity of marriage, respect for one another, and courage in tough times. We had written our own vows but had decided to keep them short, to say the rest of our vows with our life together.

Julian began, "My love, Serena Skye, I take you to be my wife, to treasure you forever, to hold you when you need me, to let you go when you need space, to honor you with my life, my words, my actions, my thoughts, and the dreams of my heart."

And I said, "Julian Rose, my only love, I take you to be my husband, to stand by your side always, to honor you with my trust, to hold you when you need me, to guard you with my life, and love you forever."

We said the *I do's*, exchanged rings, and the justice pronounced us husband and wife. He then said we could kiss. Julian lifted my veil and gently pressed his mouth on mine. I felt a fever enter my bones.

"Ladies and gentlemen," the justice went on, "Mr. and Mrs. Julian Rose."

Everybody clapped. We walked back the length of the dining room with more rose petals raining down on us and embraced again. Alberto began playing, this time singing the words of "Almost Paradise" with Tyrone. We danced, and it was the beginning of truly finding ourselves, what we were made of inside, how we would handle the darkness that was Miranda, and how we would fulfill our vows.

Carla hugged me awhile later but didn't say much. Maybe she learned something about herself that day. Cheryl was there, some wranglers who had previously worked at the ranch, our own wranglers, of course, and a few other people I didn't know. I didn't get to meet Julian's brother. When he saw me coming toward Julian in his mother's dress, he fled the room, calling later to say it wasn't right, me wearing that dress, like I had defiled it somehow. Julian said softly, "Mother would have blessed her. This is the woman she would have chosen for me."

"But she can't do that now, can she?" Jason said sharply.

"I believe she did," Julian answered, and they hung up.

I just wanted to put my hand on his chest, feel the beat of his heart, the heat of his skin. I hardly knew what was going on. He kept his arm around my waist the whole afternoon, as if fearing I might fly away, as if drawing me into himself for safekeeping. We didn't eat much of Askay's and Marta's lavish feast, but they packed some of the things to take with us. The phone rang a few times, but Julian wouldn't let anyone answer it. I know he was afraid of something Miranda might do, even though she couldn't possibly know he was getting married that day.

The afternoon faded away. The last guests had hugged us and wished us well. We changed into jeans and white turtlenecks, down pants and jackets for the drive to within a mile of the cabin. From there, Tyrone and Joe would take us on snowmobiles, as the storm had covered the trail with about six inches of white.

Soon we were out in the cold night, anxious for the warmth of the cabin and each other's arms. We clung to Joe and Tyrone as they helped us from the truck onto the snow machines. At the cabin, they unloaded our last-minute things and sped back down the trail. Askay had built a fire, and we crashed on the sofa, hands clasped.

"I tried to enjoy every single minute," Julian said, "but I just wanted to be here with you."

"I'm glad we're alone. I never liked crowds."

"We are really married," he said.

"Really married," I said. I placed my free hand on his chest like I had wanted to do all day. "You always know what I like, don't you?"

"Boy, I hope that's true," he said.

We showered and changed for the night. Angie had given me a beautiful nightgown, white of course, with lacy soft panels, thin straps, and one pearl-covered snap. Julian lay in the bed in new white sweats, his chest bare, hard-muscled, and tight. His face was devastatingly handsome in the dim light.

"Are you ready for your gift?" I asked.

"If you are ready to give it."

And I dropped the gown to the floor.

12

The morning sun broke through the sheer curtains on the east side of the canyon, but it was pretty late since the canyon walls blocked direct sunlight most of the day. We showered together and dressed in our jeans and white shirts. Luckily this desert location was near a perpetual spring, and a well had been put in years ago. We would be showering a lot.

Julian added wood to the fire and cooked breakfast, ranch-raised steak and eggs over easy. I looked at my ring. The wedding band was shaped to fit the black diamonds, curving around the bottom tip of the heart. I didn't need a ring to bind me to Julian now. Our bodies had become one, my gift to him shining like the white diamond on my hand. That diamond would be a symbol for the many *firsts* we would share.

We took a short hike up the canyon but had to turn back because of the snow, which became deeper and deeper as we climbed. We tumbled and rolled on the way down, laughing and trying to make snowballs, but the snow was too soft. We finally fell into a big hug and kissed in the cold canyon. The sun barely had time to warm our honeymoon space before it began to leave the canyon and shadows slid down the sandstone walls.

It was the honeymoon Julian had wanted all those years ago, and the honeymoon I needed to confirm my complete love for this gentle, handsome man. He was eleven years older than I was, but it didn't seem like much of a gap. We could talk about anything. We both loved old Randolph Scott movies and that Swedish film *As It*

Is in Heaven, where the sound of the voices singing at the end, while Daniel is dying, made us ache with tears. We had read many of the same books, and the writings of Derrick Jensen were high on our list, especially *A Language Older than Words*, which overwhelmed us with its beauty, sadness, and grace. It wasn't just that we liked the same things that was important, but that the emotional impact of that particular art had shaped our lives. Deeper issues found us on the same page every time. We knew a larger life was just around the bend, one where we would face pressures that could shatter the best relationships. "What do you think will get us through it?" I asked. We both said at once, "Trust."

Finally, we talked about Miranda. Julian said, "You're handling this so well, Serena, but I know what she's capable of. In the beginning, I didn't care what happened to her. I was out of my mind with grief. Then I learned more about what had been done to her, and in every scenario you could write the word *fire*. She was a victim too, and the mental illness just an added handicap, not the main cause of her instability. You don't want to know any more."

"I can imagine ... or maybe not. I always thought being around horses was dangerous, but now I think I've been astonishingly sheltered. Did you love her?" I asked cautiously.

"God ... I thought I did. I saw this energetic, pretty filly of a young woman, eager for approval, sometimes helpless and vulnerable. I was a healer ... now *I* need a healer because of Miranda's deceptions, her *choices*. It all happened so fast, her decline. One day, I think we'd been married about two months, we were hiking in the High Sierras up by South Lake. We stopped along the trail to rest. There's a little altitude there. Miranda wouldn't sit still. She walked around, kind of talking to herself. I said, *What are you doing?* And she said, *Looking for rocks that fit in my hand.* I asked, *Why?* She answered like it was a perfectly normal statement, *I was wondering how many rocks it would take to kill someone.* Stupidly, not thinking she was serious, I said, *One.* She said, *I'll remember that.*

"When we got home, she started sleeping in the guestroom, if you can call it sleeping. Night after night, she'd just pace around. Sometimes there'd be a thud against my bedroom wall. I remember the first time I locked my door. I thought, *This is the end.* Then she'd disappear for hours during the day. I tried not to look too concerned when she returned, but we'd always end up arguing. She accused me of following her or seeing another woman while she was gone. I'd say, *Miranda, you're imagining things.* That really set her off. It was just easier not to say anything. The love I had for her just kept slipping away. I spent more time with the horses. I denied that there was anything wrong. Friends would say, *I think Miranda needs help.* I didn't respond. I just waited for the *rock* in her hand. However, she chose fire in the end … two birds with one stone."

Our cabin fire was dwindling. When Julian got up to rebuild it, he pressed his hand to his chest. I said, "Julian, in March we could leave the country, go to Africa. It's a place we've both dreamed of. Askay told me he had family in Tanzania we could stay with."

"When did he say that?"

"The day after we got back from California, when the wranglers had gathered to hear about Miranda. Askay was already worried about us."

"But it's running away," Julian said. "It won't solve anything. I'd be afraid for the horses. I can't expect the boys to put their lives on the line for me."

He sat back down, hugging me, and said, "I think kissing you would be better than talking about Miranda anymore."

"I can't disagree," I said.

"I think making love to you would be even better," he said, lifting me up off the couch and heading toward the lovely white bed.

Just two days later, a blizzard rolled in across the plains and into our canyon. We heard the sound of snowmobiles buzzing off the high walls and started packing things up. Soon Mike and Tyrone were banging on the door. "Get up, you lovers! Storm's a bad one!"

There was already a foot of snow on the ground, and it was piling up fast. We could get seriously snowed in. We threw books and clothes into our backpacks and stepped into our down pants and jackets, pulling on the thick helmets the boys had brought for us and racing out into the brutal weather.

"We need to move before our tracks are completely drifted over!"

Mike shouted. And we were off, trading a quiet day in each other's arms for a wild ride down the white-choked canyon and out across the wind-scoured flats.

We were glad to be back in the security of the ranch house, with Marta and Askay hovering over us, making tea and grilled cheese sandwiches to warm us up. They were sorry we didn't get our full week at the cabin, but now we could celebrate the New Year with them. We'd have our Saturday, the first day of the year, dancing to "Almost Paradise."

"I think I'll change those words," Julian said one night. "I think I'll sing *truly paradise* from now on."

"Paraíso del Cielo Azul," I whispered.

Just then, a gust of wind cracked a cypress right in half outside by one of the cabins. The world was ghostly white and turbulent, as though the storm was deciding whom to haunt next. We couldn't see the barn, but we knew the boys were out there trying to get the range horses in, even though they didn't like to be enclosed. It would become impossible to feed them outside in the freezing gale winds. Some wouldn't find the heated water tank and die of dehydration.

Soon Tyrone trudged over to the main house and told us everything was all right. We asked him to stay and warm up, but he said one of the ranch dogs was missing, and he'd better go find her. "Okay, my man," Julian said and clapped him on the shoulder. "Don't put yourself in danger. Which dog is it?"

"The husky bitch, Sandy."

"She'll curl up someplace. Those huskies know how to survive a storm," he said, and then added to me, "That was my mom's dog. I hope we don't lose her."

For three days and nights, the storm tore up the land. We lost three steers, several more trees, and some shingles off the guest cabin roofs. Askay kept our fireplaces blazing, the big one in the living room and a smaller one in our bedroom. We all forgot New Year's Eve and hardly knew what day it was. Day and night were the same color—dark—and carried the same sounds, high winds and branches striking the house. Five feet of snow fell, unusual for our elevation in the Nevada range, not the *paradise of the blue sky* in those hours.

We were all relieved when Ty found Sandy, nose to tail, by one of the fallen trees. She was hungry and glad to be carried into the barn and fussed over. Even some of the cats rubbed their welcome on her head. Huskies notoriously chase cats, but Sandy just lay still, happily accepting the attention.

13

The weather softened, and we had a few days of sunshine. The boys got busy cleaning up the yard where they could, chopping the larger trees that had fallen into firewood, plowing paths in the snow for our trucks and a wide swath on which to unroll hay rounds for the cattle and newly turned out horses. Here and there, they cut paths to the water troughs and places where the stock could walk unimpeded.

January seemed to fly by in this manner. Julian and I went out to the barn and groomed Cielo, his grey, and others whose shaggy coats were matted with straw. We'd work on the same horse so our hands could touch over their backs, and we could talk about personal things. Behind Julian's handsome face and lean, hard body was a complex man with unresolved fears and dreams for the future that he hadn't dared to dream for years. I told Julian how I had struggled growing up estranged from my parents, sleeping in odd stables, mucking stalls for the chance to ride, watching the horses being mishandled and neglected, committing myself to making a difference in their lives, how I had to shy away from unwanted touching by flirtatious men and be strong in the face of loneliness and fear. It seemed our paths had shaped us for the healing we had found in each other's nature. We felt the blessing of the priest in our daily lives, the peace and grace he had wished for us, and put Miranda out of our minds.

But that we should not have done. In the middle of February, a month before her release date, Miranda turned into our driveway, parked quickly, and pounded on the front door. We had not seen her coming, so Julian opened the door, expecting one of the wranglers or maybe FedEx with my new dressage saddle.

I heard him say, "Miranda," and I stepped back into our bedroom, leaving the door cracked slightly. "What are you doing here?" he asked in a breaking voice.

"I came to be with my husband. I'm cured. They let me out early. Where shall I put my things?" she said, barging in.

"I thought you were going to stay with your cousin in California," Julian said, still in shock.

"Why should I do that when I have a husband in Nevada?" she said, her voice rising a notch.

"Miranda, I am not your husband," Julian said, fighting for control.

"The hell you aren't!" she cried.

Julian slowly walked over to the desk in the kitchen where he did most of the ranch business. He picked up a sheaf of papers, which happened to still be on top, and handed them to her, his divorce papers.

"This is meaningless," she said. "I didn't sign anything! You're mine! No stupid papers are going to change that!"

"Miranda, are you on medication?" Julian asked tensely.

"I was, but I can't drive with that stuff. I get sleepy. I'll start again now that I'm here."

"Miranda, you can't stay here. There's another paper there. Look. You can't come within a mile of me."

"Well, I'm never going to agree to that!" She snarled like an angry cat.

I closed the door, found Julian's cell phone, and called 911. I told the dispatcher that we had a woman with a restraining order against her in our house, that we needed help as soon as possible. Of course, technically that order wasn't good until March on her original release date, but that seemed a small matter compared to the danger we were all in.

"Who is this woman?" the lady asked.

"My husband's ex-wife. She's crazy and dangerous. Please send the sheriff to Rancho Cielo Azul."

"Right away, ma'am," she said and hung up.

I opened the door again quietly and heard Julian tell her she had to leave or he would call the authorities.

"They can't touch me! Don't you remember what happened last time?" she said with barely disguised triumph in her voice.

"I'll never forget ... but that was over fifteen years ago. Things have changed," he said calmly.

But she didn't take the hint, the apparent softer way Julian was speaking to her. She grabbed a knife from Marta's counter and started ripping the curtains at the windows. Tyrone and Joe had seen the strange car come flying down the driveway, and they now rushed into the house at the sound of raised voices.

"Who *are* you?" Joe asked, while Tyrone subdued her, barely getting the knife out of her hands.

"I am Miranda Rose!" she screamed.

"You're trespassing, lady," Tyrone told her firmly, but she returned fire.

"How can I be trespassing in my own house?"

"Because there's a restraining order against you being less than a mile from Julian and ..." He stopped, because he wasn't sure she knew anything about me, and he didn't see me in the room.

"Restraining order be damned! They can't keep me from what's mine!" She struggled against his strong hands, and then she bit his arm. He let go, yelping.

"Miranda, I beg you," Julian began. "I beg you to stop this. You're only going to be in more trouble."

"You're the one in trouble! Who does this guy think he is? I'm your wife! I don't like these curtains, so I'll take them down if I want to."

She could not be reasoned with.

Julian said, "Ty, go find Marta and have her take care of your arm."

"And who's Marta? Your whore?" she lashed out at Julian.

"She's my housekeeper, but I don't have to explain my life to you."

"I see that nice barn out there. I'll bet it's full of nice horses. I wonder how many of them could get out in a fire," she said with steel in her words.

The sound of a siren cut into Julian's fury. He just said, "I guess I won't have to find out, because you're going to be locked up!"

"The puny little jail in that town down the road isn't going to hold *me*!"

"I hope to God it does," he said.

She tried to get out the door, but Joe blocked her way. He'd put his gloves on, and she lunged and scratched to no avail. Sheriff Blake burst in and was able to handcuff the belligerent woman. She kept on yelling obscenities and threatening Julian's life.

"You owe me, you bastard! I waited fifteen years for you!"

"And I waited fifteen years for you," Julian said, shaking his head.

"I'll have *you* or you'll have *nothing!*" she screamed.

The sheriff warned her, dragging her away from Julian, "If you don't shut up, I'll tape your mouth!"

"Just try it," she challenged.

"Okay." The gray tape appeared in his hand, and he slapped a large piece over her mouth. "This stuff sure comes in handy," Blake said with a skewed smile. "Sorry for your trouble, Mr. Rose," he continued. "Can you come down to the station later and fill out a complaint?"

"Does it have to be today?" Julian asked.

"That would be best," the sheriff replied.

"I'll call in a while. I'm not feeling too well right now." His face was white.

"I understand, Mr. Rose," he said and jerked Miranda out the door. "I'll send someone back for her car."

"Thanks," was all Julian could say.

I was beside him the instant the door closed. I said, "Julian, I'll kill her before I let her hurt you!"

"You'll never get the chance. She's too smart."

"How could they let her go without telling you?"

"Maybe they tried. The phone lines were down in January, remember, and I changed my cell phone number. I was afraid Miranda would get it. Apparently she didn't need that to find the ranch. She seems to bypass the usual means of communication, so you don't know she's there until it's too late," he said, stumbling on the words.

"Julian, will you let me call the institution and find out what happened, what we're supposed to do? I couldn't really *kill* her, you know."

"I know, Serena. Neither could I. But somebody has to see what a danger she is. Somebody has to listen to me."

He wasn't a man to cry, but through real tears he described the day Miranda had burned up two of his finest horses trapped in his horse trailer. She didn't deny it. She said he cared more about them than he did her. "I guess it was pretty true at the time," Julian admitted, "but no matter, it was the end for us. I didn't buy any more horses for a long time."

Marta was taking down the ruined curtains. The sound of Miranda's voice lingered in the air.

Julian went on, "Soon after she went to the medical center for evaluation, she came back to kill me. She had been hiding all her pills and faked a miraculous recovery. The staff of that place was glad to see her go, never mind she had committed a horrendous criminal act."

He closed his eyes, either to see or not see what happened next. He spoke the words in a rush.

"I was in my bedroom. It was dark, and so the bullet missed me. She had my gun, and she was a good shot. I had taught her well. We struggled with the weapon, and I overpowered her. I tied her to the bedpost, and she had chewed halfway through the rope by the time the police arrived."

Julian seemed to breathe easier, being able to tell the story at last. Some color had come back into his face. But he put his hands against his chest and bent over slightly, saying, "It's double the pain now, because she could hurt *you*."

"She doesn't know about me," I said, putting my arms around him.

"She'll hear about you, in town, somewhere. You're not exactly a secret."

"If only I could bear this pain for you."

"Serena, your love has no bounds."

"You could say that."

He straightened up, but he was still trembling from the confrontation and the dark possibilities we faced.

"I'll go with you to town," I said.

"Maybe … we'll see."

The phone rang. Sheriff Blake pleaded with Julian to come file charges. They could only hold her for twenty-four hours for the original complaint.

"How many charges would you need to keep her locked up forever?" Julian asked.

"How many charges we talkin' about here, Mr. Rose?"

"Oh, well, trespassing, property damage, illegal possession of a weapon, defying a court-ordered restraint, threatening me and my livestock, let's see, there must be more."

"I get the picture," the sheriff said. "Just get down here as soon as you can."

"Do you have to go now?" I asked.

"Pretty soon, love."

"Will you let me drive you in?"

"That would put you right in the middle of it," he answered.

"I'm already in the middle of it. I vowed to guard you with my life."

"I thought that was a bit extreme at the time," he said with a brief smile.

Just then, Marta stood by us with two glasses of the *fever cocktail*. "I thought this help," she said.

"I guess Serena and I need our meds too," he said. "Thanks, Marta. I don't know what I'd do without you."

"I not as old as Miss Serena when I help bring you into the world. I not let crazy woman hurt you!"

We sat at the kitchen table and sipped the tranquilizing juice. The ripped curtains were gone, and Marta was busy looking through her collection of material for something suitable to replace them. "Oh, look!" she cried out. "Here is print with horses, greys and blacks!"

"That's the one," Julian said.

I took one of his hands and kissed his cool fingertips, marveling at how I loved every part of his body. "I think I know a way out of this, Julian. Will you trust me?" I said.

"With my life," he answered.

For weeks I had been trying to figure ways to subdue Miranda and shift her out of our lives, ever since Julian's stressful time in California. My best idea was probably going to be the hardest. My chance came before I was really ready—about an hour after Sheriff Blake's first call. Miranda had slipped out a bathroom window with the gun she had taken from the female officer, whom she left tied to a pipe behind the toilet with the woman's belt.

Julian had pressed the speaker button when the second call came so we could hear the news together.

"Piece of work, that one," Blake said. "She found her car. We hadn't removed the keys after takin' the car from your place. She's prob'ly headed your way … wait a minute … what the …" He sputtered to a stop. We could hear faint radio noise. Julian leaned against the counter and closed his eyes. The sheriff spoke again suddenly, excitement rising in his voice. "She ran out of gas at the crossroads! An officer on his way back in from patrol says he saw her get out of the car. He chased her on foot, but she fired on him and the bullet lodged in his shoulder! Drove himself to the hospital and just called in. I'm sending some guys out!"

"You'll never find her," Julian said. "I'll have to go on horseback."

"I don't think I can allow that, Mr. Rose."

"What did you say, sheriff? You're breaking up." Julian ended the conversation and looked at me grimly. "Get ready for the ride of your life," he said.

14

The sun was still fairly high when we cantered out across the ranch toward the crossroads. Julian had a scoped rifle in its scabbard, and I had my lariat. We had each other and a few hours of daylight to find Miranda before she froze to death in the unforgiving desert night. We had to keep her from reaching the ranch. Too many lives were at stake. There seemed to be no question that we had to do it together. Once Julian said, "You should go back Serena. This is my fight."

"Not anymore," I said and kept my horse in that ground-covering trot at my husband's side. It was already down to ten degrees, and there were no clouds in sight. Clearer meant colder. And there was not much shelter in that part of the territory.

"Julian, I think we should separate. If she starts shooting wildly at one of us from a distance, the other can get behind her, maybe at least confuse her. She doesn't know the land like we do."

"Let's ride along either side of that low ridge before we break into the open," Julian said, breathing heavily. "It runs on an angle toward the crossroads. If we see her, I'll ride ahead of you. I don't want you in her sights."

"Okay," I agreed, feeling helpless and beat. I thought, *Miranda, Miranda, I'm stopping you in your tracks!*

Julian loped his grey down one line of the ridge. Watching him in the saddle just made my heart ache. *We should just let her freeze tonight*, I thought, moving in a zigzag pattern around cactus and lone pines and junipers. Julian was more exposed, and he began calling her name. The warmth of the sun was diminishing, as were our chances of finding Miranda before dark.

I was still on the same side of the ridge when I heard a shot and saw that Julian was off his horse, leading him toward the far end of the ridge where a butte called Towering Peak stuck up into the fading light. I dismounted and tied the buckskin to a stiff creosote bush and grabbed my lariat. I crawled through a crack in the eroded ridge and saw Miranda walk around the end, about a quarter mile away.

Julian was yelling, "Miranda! Put the gun down! Let's talk!"

I couldn't hear her answer. I couldn't hear Julian anymore. But there were no more gunshots. I moved closer to the place where she had disappeared. The sound of Julian's horse shuffling through the sand kept my footsteps muffled, and soon I could hear everything they said. They were ten feet from me on the other side of Towering Peak.

"Miranda, please, if you ever loved me, put down the gun!" Julian's voice cut through the chilling night air.

"Of course I loved you! But you spent more time with those damn horses!"

"Miranda, you didn't stay home. I never knew where you were, off with those crazy girlfriends, doing who knows what! You knew when you married me I wasn't a *party guy*. I didn't drink, and I didn't do drugs, and—"

She cut him off. "Your drugs were your horses, and maybe the damn girlie barrel racers! I never had a chance!"

"Maybe you're right, Miranda." He sounded defeated. "But if you want a chance now, you'll have to put down the gun."

"Fifteen years! Fifteen years, and you'll give me a chance now?" she raved.

"I don't want to die," he said.

She fired. I thought he was pretty close to her now. It would have been an easy shot, but the bullet zinged off a rock nearby.

"I can do better than that!" she cried, and I could imagine her lifting her arm again.

I stepped forward, swung the rope, and pinned her arms to her legs, cinching the noose as tight as I could. She could still fire the gun, but her range was severely limited and included her own feet. Julian backed his horse down the butte and tied him out of danger. Miranda stamped her feet and twisted her wrists, trying to get control of the weapon. I came hand over hand along the rope, keeping it as restrictive as I could. I waved Julian away, saying, "Give me a minute."

Finally the woman turned her head, still not understanding what held her fast. She followed the line of the lariat to my hands and then laid her head back and screamed. The ferocious sound split the air and galloped off on waves of its own across the desert. She shot the gun twice, directly into the ground. I didn't flinch.

"Miranda!" I shouted. She stared up at the butte and then back toward the highway. She'd only gotten about a mile from her car.

"Miranda! Look at me!"

She turned her head but glared at the white sand.

"Look me in the eyes!" I commanded.

"Julian!" she screeched.

"No, Miranda, he's not in this circle. Look at *me*."

"Who are you?"

"I'm the one with the rope."

"But who *are* you?"

"I'll tell you later. Right now I need you to hear me."

She stopped squirming. I loosened the rope just slightly. Then she really looked at me.

"I want Julian!" she cried. "I don't want you!"

"Yes, you do."

"Why?"

"Because I'm going to help you," I said as truthfully as I could.

"You can't help me!" she screamed.

"I can … and I will, but you have to let me. First, drop the gun."

She wrenched herself wildly against the rope, trying to free her hand.

I tightened the rope.

"Hurt, hurt!" she yelled.

"Drop the gun, Miranda. You don't need it."

She whimpered and squirmed but loosened her grip on the gun. I loosened the rope. The gun fell to the ground. I slackened the rope completely and flung the loop over her head. She faced me, but her eyes flashed left and right. I coiled the rope and slapped it against my thigh. Her eyes locked on mine.

"Good girl," I said, and then, "I'm going to kick the gun away, Miranda, but you keep your eyes on me, okay?"

"Okay."

I walked toward her cautiously, saying softly, "It's okay, Miranda, it's okay. Trust me" like I would to a frightened horse. Miranda had the gun at her feet; the horse has his one thousand pound body and long, lethal legs with which to strike without warning. Even a small healing, a bit of earned trust doesn't always come easily or safely.

"Are you in pain?" I asked as I booted the gun out of her reach.

"Pain, yes, lots of pain," she answered shakily.

"Do you know why?"

"Can't find Julian!" she said having a hard time keeping her eyes on me.

"Miranda, do you have any medication in your bag?"

"Yes."

"If you take it, I will show you Julian."

She looked at me with disbelief.

"Just try it, Miranda. I want to teach you something."

She stared at me uncomprehending, shivering in the deepening cold, fighting the voices in her head that told her I was the enemy. But finally she dug around in her backpack and swallowed a couple of pills. I waved to Julian, and he stepped out from behind the butte. Miranda gasped and held out her arms.

"Miranda, he's still not in this circle. You can't touch him."

"Why, why?" She stamped her feet again but looked at me for the answer.

"You broke the law. This is the lesson: life—yours, mine, Julian's, the sheriff's, your doctor's—is a two-way street." *There are probably more streets than that,* I thought, *but right now I would be happy if she just could see two.* "Say that, Miranda. Say *two-way street,*" I urged her.

"Two-way street! Two-way street!"

"Good girl. Now listen. This is what it means. You are not the only one in pain. I am in pain, because you threatened someone I love."

She started to protest.

"Wait … Julian is in pain, because his parents died in a plane crash not too long ago."

"Oh, no, I didn't know. That's bad, very bad." She was beginning to consider things outside herself.

I went on, "The sheriff has pain, because you didn't follow the rules, and you hurt one of his officers. You have pain, because you have an illness that has damaged you. It's not fair, but think *two-way street*. Think, *If I face some of my pain, people will back off, not pile more pain on me. If I follow the law, the sheriff will leave me alone.* You get that?"

"Maybe."

"You don't have to remember all of that, just remember *two-way street*. You can control what happens to you. You can give up some of your demands, your hysteria, and someone will give you a little more freedom. Nobody gets everything she wants … listen to me. I'm in love with Julian, and you are hurting him."

"Julian's mine! My husband!"

"No, he's not, but he can give you a gift, maybe a place to live rent-free, money, and a way to receive your medicines."

"It's a trick, a trick!" She was losing it again.

"It's not a trick."

"What do I have to do?" she asked warily.

"This home, this money, these meds, may not be given in the state of Nevada."

"Why?"

"Because it's against the law. We are all breaking the law right now in this circle. You have a paper that says you cannot come within one mile of Julian or me."

"That's not right! He's my husband!"

"No, Miranda. He's my husband."

She came at me with teeth bared like a mountain lion. I swung the lariat and jerked it tight around her, and she writhed to the ground, clawing at the rope.

"Miranda … you didn't remember the two-way street. You give, I give. You have to trust that."

"*I don't trust anyone!*" she raged.

"You can trust me," I said.

"Nooooooo ..."

"Yes, you *can* trust me. Try standing up and looking into my eyes," I said. I motioned to Julian to move out of sight.

Miranda struggled to her feet and looked at me. I released the lariat.

"Now for the big one. Listen, Miranda. Listen carefully. You choose to go with the sheriff tonight."

She shook her head, her dark hair flailing around her ragged face.

"Say you will, Miranda."

"I ... will," she said, softly, testing.

I said, "Julian, come over here and put your arms around Miranda."

He gasped, "No."

"Julian. I mean it. Now."

He came into the circle of my tentative trust with his ex-wife and held her reluctantly, but it was enough. She looked back at me and said, "I give. You give. Two-way street." Then she began trudging resolutely across the frozen plain, one of Julian's hands in hers. I walked a ways with them.

Miranda was chanting in a loud voice, "Two-way street ... two-way street."

I whispered to Julian, "Don't let go. Tell her she has to do her part. Tell her if she'll take her meds tomorrow, I'll come see her the next day."

"Serena?"

"You've got to do it, whatever it takes. You're in the circle now. I'm going back for the horses ... and the gun."

I watched them with my heart in my throat. It wasn't over. I needed more to diffuse Miranda, but I had no idea what that might be. I was working in the dark on this one. Off in the distance, I saw the red lights, no sirens, of two sheriff vehicles heading our way. Soon, Miranda was placed, without handcuffs, in the back of one of the patrol cars, and it sped off toward town. Julian looked sick, but he clasped my shoulders and divined some relief from my eyes.

"That was amazing," he said.

"Not so amazing," I told him. "Just a wild horse in the round pen for the first time."

15

We sat on the edge of the highway as the sun plunged down the indigo sky. We leaned against each other, grateful for silence. It wasn't too long before we saw Tyrone coming down the highway with the rig to take us home. Nothing else moved in the twilight.

We loaded the horses, climbed in the warm truck, and tried to tell Ty what happened. "You've never seen a round pen act like what Serena just did," Julian was saying.

"Some horses don't make it," the foreman said.

"At least she tried," I said.

"I heard of a horse once that had to be put down. He tried to kill people," Ty continued.

"I've never had a horse like that in the round pen," I said.

"There's always a first," Tyrone reminded me.

It was Saturday, and all the boys were in the main house eating Askay's cinnamon tilapia. They stood when we came in. They seemed not to know whether to clap or cry, but relief showed clearly on their faces.

"Serena put her in the round pen," Ty said, "with no rail but the sky."

Then they clapped and cheered, and I thought, *This is a human being we're talking about*, and felt guilty. "The only reason I did it was to save Julian's life," I told them. "Don't expect a repeat performance."

Then I thought, *I got in the round pen with Miranda. I had to stay. There was no question of not seeing it through.*

"Will they keep her locked up?" Alberto asked.

"We have to go file charges," Julian explained. "But I don't know if they'll send her back to California. She's here illegally. God, just breathing is illegal for her! She broke the law in Nevada, so the state might want to keep her. She's a genius at breaking out, as we all know now. There doesn't seem to be a clear course for her life, but I doubt it's in the round pen. The first time you opened the gate, she'd be gone."

Julian and I ate a few vegetables and a swallow or two of Marta's fever cocktail. Alberto asked us if we wanted the song tonight, and we both said, gratefully, "Yes." Lara and Gayle were back early for their ranch jobs, so everyone danced. Billy hung on our every move. We felt eaten alive by the events of the day, but we longed for the song and its promising words. Julian never took his eyes from mine.

Almost paradise. We're knocking on heaven's door. How could we ask for more? I swear that I can see forever in your eyes. Paradise.

On Monday, Julian and I walked into the police station. An officer rushed up to us and said, "We're having some trouble with the prisoner. She keeps yelling, *Two-way street! Two-way street!* We have to handcuff her for her to use the ladies' room, and she won't eat. She just throws the food all over her cell."

"Have you offered her her meds?" I asked.

"Uh … no. I don't know where they are," he stuttered.

"They're in her backpack. For heaven's sake, the woman needs help."

"That's what she keeps shouting. *Help me, help me, help me,* over and over."

"Let me see her," I said.

Julian declined to go with me.

Her cell was a mess. Everyone was afraid of her. "Miranda," I called as soon as I thought she could hear me.

She cried out, "Two-way street! Two-way street!"

"That's right," I said. "I'll help you."

She was handcuffed to the bars.

"Somebody get her backpack and unlock these cuffs."

"Against the rules, miss," the officer stated, beginning to turn away.

"I don't care. Do it!"

I searched through Miranda's jumbled pack and found some Thorazine. I figured half a dose would take the edge off, so I gave it to her, holding the key for the cuffs. "I'll unlock these, and then you'll swallow the pill—okay?"

She nodded. This was pushing the system a bit. You don't give the horse a carrot *before* he lets you halter him. *Well, there may be exceptions,* I thought. When she took the pill, I said, "Good girl."

She cried a little, an abused little mare caught in the barbed fence, no one going to her with the wire cutters. I studied her. I could see how she might have been pretty once. She had dark, dark eyes and brunette hair streaked with gray, like mine, but with more attractive contrast. Her skin was surprisingly smooth and unblemished, although she must have been about forty. Of course, her nails were chipped from clawing at everything in sight, but she was slender and provocative. I could see how Julian might have fallen for her fifteen years ago.

"Miranda, do you know what's going to happen today?"

"No."

"And she's not going to hear it from you," said a snippy little court-appointed defender named Alexander Suel, approaching the cell.

"Why not? I'm the only thing she's got going for her," I said, not releasing Miranda's hand where she gripped mine through the bars.

"You're the one who charged her!"

"Actually, I'm not," I said. "That would be my husband. Julian Rose."

"Same thing," he said bitingly.

"Miranda, do you want me to leave you?"

"No, no, no, no, no, no, two-way street, two-way street."

"Oh, my God, what kind of lunatic is this?"

I slapped him hard. Miranda giggled and squeezed my hand.

"And what kind of defense attorney are you to treat her with such disrespect?"

"Hey, she's all yours, lady," he spit out. He hurried away.

"Miranda, I need to talk to the sheriff. Are you okay by yourself for a minute?"

She nodded, *yes.* The meds were helping. When a horse enters the round pen, you're supposed to start from scratch. That wouldn't be possible with Miranda. Her mental illness was a factor I couldn't control with all my talk of *two-way streets* and releasing the pressure on her shattered mind. I had to find a way to *train* her out of Julian's life.

I went up to Sheriff Blake. "Would you be willing to handcuff her to me on the way over to court? She has no defense lawyer and barely knows what's going on. I got her to take her meds. It's chancy, but she'll never go with one of you."

"I don't like it, Mrs. Rose," he replied. "She scared my deputy so bad, she quit her job!"

"I know. She scares me too, but she trusts me more than she's trusted anyone for years. I'm doing it for Julian."

"She's required to have an attorney," he said.

"Is there a woman available?"

He sighed. "I'll try to locate Barbara Wells. She's good."

"Okay. I'll tell Miranda."

I went back to the cell. She jumped up and reached for me. I took her hands through the bars.

"What's your name?" she asked.

"Serena."

"Serena what?" she persisted.

"Serena Rose."

Her eyes brightened, and she said, "Just like mine! Miranda *Rose.* Just like mine."

"Yes." I guess I couldn't take that away from her.

"Miranda, we're going to practice the *two-way street.*"

"How?" she asked.

"I'm going to let the sheriff handcuff you to *me,* so we can walk over to the courthouse—okay?"

"Okay."

"Then we're going to meet a woman who will help you with the legal stuff."

"Don't know her, don't want her," she whined.

"If you won't accept the lawyer, you'll have to be cuffed to one of those men over there and maybe have your legs shackled," I explained.

"I'll have the lawyer," she said quickly.

"Good girl."

She smiled. *Oh, God, if only someone had put her in the round pen years ago,* I thought.

I found Julian sitting alone in the back of the courtroom, his head in his hands.

"Are you okay, love?"

"Barely," he replied.

I told him what I was going to do. He hated it.

"Julian, what would you have thought of me if I had walked away from the roan mare before I got her in the trailer?"

"I would have thought you were smart," he said.

"But knowing the outcome, does that give you faith in the process?"

"Yes … it does."

"I think I have to do this. I got Miranda to agree to a lawyer and let them handcuff her to the table after the proceedings start. She sees the two-way street."

"Where did *that* idea come from anyway?" he asked.

"I don't know. I just made it up out there in the desert, in desperation."

"You're a genius." Julian kissed my hands.

Spectators were crowding into the room. They had heard about Miranda's tantrums and the scene on the ranch. Miranda was not going to like this. The deal did not include a group of strangers.

I went back to the jail. Barbara Wells greeted me and said, "I think I need some background before I agree to take this case."

"It's complicated," I said.

"Apparently so," she said. "I'm good at complicated."

"Okay." I told her that Miranda was married to Julian Rose in California over fifteen years ago, that her mental illness surfaced about that time and was not treated, that she had killed two of his horses and tried to kill him with a gun he had taught her how to use, how he finally had her committed for evaluation, supported her, and waited for fifteen years, but she didn't get better, how he had divorced her, without her consent, and married me last Christmas. "In February, she wormed her way out of the institution that was preparing to release her in March. Mr. Rose has a restraining order against her."

"Yes, I see that here," Miss Wells said.

I continued, "She came straight to Julian's ranch and started threatening everyone, including Julian's stable full of fantastic and expensive horses."

"In what way, threatened?"

"To burn the barn down."

"Isn't that how she killed his two horses? I see a document charging her with animal cruelty."

"Yes … it's a very painful memory for Julian to this day," I told her.

"Mrs. Rose, why on earth are you helping her?"

"I work with abused and troubled horses. It seemed like a job I could do. Besides, Julian and I were out in the desert a few nights ago with Miranda and a gun. I didn't have too many options."

"I shouldn't ask you this, being Miranda's attorney, but what do you want out of this?"

"I want Miranda to get help but be safely and completely out of our lives. This whole thing is tearing my husband apart. The thing is, I've started a dialogue with Miranda, and it's working. I feel that I can't walk away, but for my husband's sake, I have to find another avenue. I agreed to be handcuffed to her if she'd let you represent her."

Barbara Wells seemed to consider all this carefully. I felt she was a reasonable person, but a defense lawyer, after all, so I didn't have much hope. In a few minutes, Miranda and I were escorted into the courtroom linked together. Julian did not look up. This was a round pen he did not want to be anywhere near.

The judge said, "What is the meaning of this?"

Barbara Wells said, "I can explain, Your Honor."

"It better be good!"

"Good, good, good Miranda," the accused woman said. She began to fidget.

"Two-way street," I whispered.

"Keep your client quiet, Miss Wells," the judge said.

"Your Honor, I … this is a very unusual case."

"That may be, but I will have order in my courtroom."

The prosecutor read the charges that Julian had made.

Miranda said, "No, no, no, no, no."

I said, "Miranda. It's not your turn." She closed her mouth.

The judge looked at me. "Ma'am, who are you?"

"My name is Serena," I said.

"Last name?" he sighed.

"Rose."

"Are you related to the defendant?"

"No."

"Are you involved in the charges?"

I really didn't know how to answer, but Miss Wells jumped in, to her credit.

"Your Honor, Serena Rose has developed a relationship, a trust, with the defendant that enabled us to be in this courtroom. My client has mental problems. Serena has encouraged my client to take her meds. I now ask that she be uncuffed, and Miranda cuffed to the table, as my client agreed to do."

"Officer, proceed," the judge ordered.

Miranda looked at me, her eyes full of fear and confusion.

"I'll sit right behind you, Miranda. You can do this," I told her.

There was a tense moment when I moved back, and Miranda was re-cuffed to the long, mahogany table, but she let Barbara Wells pat her on the shoulder, a *good girl* move, which I was grateful for. The woman really got it.

Then the charges were read again.

"Miss Wells, how does your client plead?" the judge asked.

"Not guilty, by reason of mental defect," Barbara answered.

"No!" Miranda screamed.

"Miss Wells, you must control your client!"

Barbara turned and begged Miranda to be quiet, saying that things would get worse if she wouldn't. Then Miss Wells went on, "My client doesn't know where she is. She believes she's still married to Mr. Julian Rose, on whose property she was apprehended by, I will admit, questionable means. There's a restraining order against her, stating that she must stay one mile from the man she thinks is her husband. She maintains she hasn't seen this document until now. She was recently discharged from the Institute for Better Mental Health in California, a place she had been for over fifteen years. She has no idea how to behave in society and needs guidance. Serena Rose, at great danger to herself, stepped in to ease my client's fears."

"Your Honor," the prosecutor broke in. "All that is beside the point. Miranda Rose broke the law. She has a record of threatening people, even threatening the woman sitting behind her right now, the *wife* of Julian Rose."

With the word *wife*, which Barbara Wells had avoided, Miranda leapt from her chair and dragged the table halfway across the room before she was contained. "*I* am Julian's wife!" she wailed.

I should have given her the full dose of Thorazine, I thought, glancing back at Julian. He seemed relieved that Miranda had been hustled out of the room.

The judge was banging his gavel. "I will have order in this courtroom!" he boomed.

And then it was over, because the judge said, "Miranda Rose is obviously not competent. I accept the plea of *not guilty by reason of mental defect,* but I will require a psychiatric examination at the Nevada State Women's Prison before I turn her loose on the world."

At that, Julian stood and said, so softly that the judge had to ask him to repeat it, "She'll be out of there in less than a week."

"All right, everyone in my chambers," he ordered, "in five minutes."

Julian met me in the middle of the aisle with that heartbreaking look in his eyes. He put his arms around me and laid his head against mine. "You did everything you could," he said. "More than I ever would have, but then you have a big heart. I didn't look at the past for fifteen years. Well, I guess that's not completely true. I did try to get a divorce eight years ago. Now I have to relive the whole mess all over again. Holding you is the only thing that makes any sense."

"It seems that way to me too," I said.

"And we made sense from day one," he added.

"My life suddenly made sense to me that day, anyway."

"Maybe we should go to Africa," he admitted.

"Here's the thing, Julian. If Miranda wasn't who she was, and I didn't know what she'd done, I'd stay with her in the round pen until I fixed it. So I have to disregard those fifteen years, as I did the roan's flailing around outside the horse trailer, if I'm any good at all. I have to stay with Miranda."

"She's so dangerous, Serena, like that horse Ty heard about who tried to *kill* people."

"I know. I was reminded of that when I was handcuffed to her. With an unfixable horse, at least you have a chance to climb out of the arena, not stand there attached by a rope!"

We made our way to the judge's chambers through a crowd of townspeople and reporters asking a barrage of questions, most of which we had no answers for. Barbara Wells and the prosecutor were already there, and a court reporter.

"Please, be seated," the judge said. "First, I will address Mr. Rose. Sir, why do you think your ex-wife can get out of the women's prison?"

"She's escaped from so many other more difficult situations, right from this jail. That minimum security place will be a piece of cake for her."

"We have a reputable psychiatric hospital in the same town. Could she go there?" the judge asked.

"Those hospitals don't want to keep her long term, and she's smart enough to take her meds and appear sane enough to be released. I think, Your Honor, she has to be treated like a hard criminal. I know it doesn't seem fitting for the crime of trespassing or ignoring the restraining order, but I have to protect my wife, my employees, my horses, and my property. If I believed in vigilante justice, she'd be dead. I watched my wife tame her briefly like a wild horse, but you saw Miranda's strength and a bit of her madness. Even a wild horse wouldn't behave that way after given a warm barn in a storm."

Then the judge turned to Miss Wells. "And what is your opinion, counselor?"

"When I was alone with her, after they uncuffed Serena, Miranda kept whispering to me, *My husband is here. See him? See him? He'll help me, watch, watch,* mumbling on and on about a two-way street and a barn full of horses. *He'd better help me, he'd better,* she'd say, and then, *If he didn't have those horses, he'd love me more.* She's not in the real world, Your Honor, and she is truly dangerous. My only defense of her is that she's mentally ill. But my answer, frankly, is that she needs to be locked up. Treatment maybe. But no chance to get out and harm these good people."

"Thank you, Miss Wells," he said. "Mr. Prosecutor?"

"Well, I agree with Barbara for the first time in my career. I'd lock Miranda up and, at least, hide the key," he said vehemently.

"And Serena Rose, you are Julian's wife?"

"Yes."

"May I ask why you allowed yourself to be cuffed to the defendant?"

"I've never fled the round pen, Your Honor," I said.

"What the hell does that mean?" he asked, and turned to the reporter. "That's off the record. The *hell*, not her answer."

"It means I saw this crazed woman, who was abused and scared, and I thought I could take the edge off, make her understand there was a better way for her," I answered.

"Are you a psychologist?" he asked.

"No, Your Honor."

"Yes, she is," Julian broke in. "You should see her with a troubled horse."

"With all due respect, Mr. Rose, your ex-wife is not a troubled horse, as fitting as that image might be," the judge said.

I said, without much hope, "I'd like to see Miranda one more time."

"No!" several voices spoke at once.

But the judge looked at me soberly and said, "What will you do?"

"I don't know yet. It depends on Miranda."

"You must have an officer with you," he said.

"No … there can't be any distractions. Just give me twenty minutes or so."

"Against my better judgment, I'm going to let you do it, but I'll be watching through the one-way glass. Miss Wells?"

"Yes, I'll be there."

"Mr. Kellner?"

"I wouldn't miss this for the world," the prosecutor replied.

The judge asked his court officer to set it up.

Julian would not let go of my hand, almost holding me back from the room where I would be alone with his ex-wife. "You know I don't like this," he said, trying to dissuade me from my last chance with Miranda.

"This may take a lariat of love," I said and walked through the door.

16

When they brought Miranda into the bleak room that had only two chairs welded to the floor, I was waiting in one of them. I said to her, "Will you talk to me?"

She nodded. I told the guard to remove the cuffs. Miranda said, "Thank you."

I gently rubbed one of her wrists that had a bruise from the cuffs and said, "Do you know where you are?"

"In Nevada."

"Yes, but why?"

"I came to find Julian," she answered, her voice rising.

"What if you could never find him?" I asked.

"I'd kill myself," she said evenly.

"And what if you did find him, and he was married to someone else?"

Her eyes narrowed. "Like you," she said.

"Like me."

"I'd kill him and all his horses."

"And then what would you have?"

"Nothing!" she shrieked, and then seemed to yield. "But I already have nothing, so what difference does it make?"

I noticed that she didn't include me in the slaughter, so I said, "You have me."

She thought about that for a minute and then said, "You hate me."

"I don't hate you, Miranda. I want to help you. If you can't have

Julian, you could have me. I would come see you. I would make sure you had the best care, the best meds, the best room, with all the things you like to eat and touch and see."

Suddenly something hit me like a range horse jumped by a puma.

"Did you know that Julian's mother was an artist?"

She shook her head. "Dead now. Dead now."

"Miranda, I could get you one of her watercolors for your room."

"You could?"

"Yes, but you could never see Julian again. He would be lost to you. Two-way street, Miranda."

"You would come see me?"

"Only if you follow the rules of the house where you live."

"You would come see me if I gave up Julian?"

"Yes."

"You're just saying that so I'll go away."

"It's true that I want you to go away from Julian. But I also want to help you be a better Miranda, a Miranda who takes her meds and doesn't hurt people. Can you understand that?"

"I think so ... I'm trying."

"Good girl."

Had twenty minutes passed? I didn't know, but nobody opened the door, so I went on. "Miranda, if you agree to go to the hospital or a place where you might have to live the rest of your life, I'll go to the ranch and bring back one of the paintings. The paintings are very precious to Julian. You'll have a piece of Julian's heart, but you have to give up your freedom."

"I can have the picture today?"

"Yes."

"And you'll visit me?"

"How about once a month?" I suggested.

"Okay. Bring the picture. I want the picture!"

"Good girl, Miranda," I said, fighting tears.

When I returned to the room behind the glass window, Julian took my face in his hands. There were tears in his eyes too. He said, "Thank you ... thank you."

The judge said, "If I ever have a problem with a horse, I'm bringing it to you, Serena Rose."

Barbara Wells said, "I'll find the right facility for her. Would you like to research this with me, Mr. Kellner?" And they left together.

Julian said, "It will be hard to lose a painting, but I have to give too."

"We'll choose it together," I said. "We'll find the perfect thing. Your mother will save us, even from the grave."

"It was brilliant, Serena. I have hope for the first time. What made you think of that?"

"It was simple, really. I looked around that awful, dark gray room and thought, *If I had to be here forever, what would I want?* Helen's watercolors came immediately to mind. I wasn't sure it would work with Miranda, but then I wasn't sure the roan mare would go in the trailer either."

We stood in the living room at the ranch, gazing at Helen's paintings. We sought the one that would keep Miranda out of our lives. I would visit her, but never tell Julian the days I went to wherever Miranda would be. I would still be in the round pen; Julian would be on a different part of the range.

It was so hard choosing that picture. It was not only difficult to give one of them up, but also to find the right one for a damaged soul. There was a sketch of a horseman carrying a newborn calf out of a storm.

"I remember that," Julian said. "The calf was pretty strong, but it didn't struggle in my arms. The mom followed me in. Look, there's just the suggestion of a cow in my horse's tracks a ways behind."

"Oh no, she can't have that one," I cried.

The ranch scenes, which were beautiful to us, would have no meaning for Miranda. We wandered around feeling somewhat helpless. Helen would know which one to give. Then, hanging in a corner by the bookcase, we were startled to see a bold painting, strong brush strokes, deep colors, a sharp vision of a stiff-legged, young horse in the round pen awaiting its fate, the dark hide shining with sweat. His eyes were rolled back, whites showing. Cowboys lined the rails. They had whips and spurs and lariats, their hats pulled down over their faces, their lips set. And there, through the lower two rails, a hand reached out. There was the intimation of some kind of treat, a piece of carrot, a stem of hay. Julian put his hand over his heart.

"Serena," he said, choking up. "That's my mother's arm. She painted herself into that picture. She knew there was a better way. The rest of us hadn't figured that out. This one was meant for Miranda. I know it as sure as I'm standing here. I swear I didn't see my mother's hand until today."

"It's perfect, Julian. Miranda will get it. She'll love it. It will be a healing every time she looks at it. Can you relinquish it?"

"For you, for our life, yes."

We took the painting down and wrapped it carefully. I would be the one to see Miranda unwrap it, but it would be a healing for Julian and for me too.

We drove back to the town jail, and I went into the room where Miranda was locked up with the painting under my arm. She brightened when she saw me and cried, "Serena, Serena, I took my meds!"

"Good girl, Miranda. I've brought you the best painting Julian had. Here." And I set the package in her outstretched hands.

She looked directly into my eyes. "No one has ever given me a gift like this," she said and tore off the wrapping. The painting took on its own life in the bare room.

"Oh, oh, oh," she whispered. She placed a finger on the signature, *Helen Rose.*

"That is Julian's mother, Miranda."

She studied the scene, seeming to enjoy the dark strokes, the white in the eyes of the frightened horse, and then her eyes shifted to the arm offering the gift through the cowboys' rigid stares and means of torture.

"That's Helen's hand, Miranda. She painted herself in the picture. It's the only time she ever did that."

Tears rolled down Miranda's cheeks. "I wish I had known her," she said in a whisper.

"I wish I had known her too," I said.

"When I hang it in my room, will you come see me?" she asked.

"I will … I promise."

"This picture will save me," she said, "just like the wild horse in the pen."

I thought, *I hope to God no one ever takes that picture away from her.* And then I touched her arm that cradled the painting, even though I was told we couldn't have any contact, and said, "Good girl, Miranda. Good girl."

She was led down a dark corridor clutching the beautiful picture, the best of Helen's work, the hardest for Julian to let go. I sat there alone for a few minutes. I imagined Miranda carrying Helen's painting from room to room, cell to cell, hanging it devotedly on some stark lodging wall where she could see that glimpse of Julian's life, that glimpse that could be, ultimately, better than any medication—his mother's hand reaching out to her through the bars.

At last, I rushed out to Julian's loving arms. We sat in the truck, unable to speak. He put a CD in my hands, a recording of "Almost Paradise," but I didn't have to play it right then. The lines were written on my heart.

Almost paradise. We're knocking on heaven's door. How could we ask for more? Now we hold the future in our hands. Almost paradise … paradise.

PART TWO

1

When I was thirty-five, I had Julian's son, a fine boy we named Robert Henry Askay Rose. Robert was my maternal grandfather. He and my grandmother had given me a place to crash when I was thirteen, no questions asked. Our boy would be called Hank from the beginning. It fit.

The crazy thing was that he was born in the round pen, literally. I knew my water had broken but thought I could get two more horses done before I had to leave for the hospital. Julian wasn't happy with me still working so close to my due date, but I had quit riding months before and only took the easy horses for ground work. So that day, I handed Tyrone the Paint I was teaching to accept the body blanket and fell to my knees. Ty yelled for Julian, and he and Marta came running just as little Hank decided to launch himself into the world. They carried me to the truck after cutting the cord with Julian's knife, and Hank and I were rushed to the emergency room.

A few hours later, we were back at the ranch with Hank in the very crib where Helen had laid Julian in the canyon house. Julian didn't want to sleep but pulled his easy chair over to the tiny bed and stared with awe at his newborn son. He didn't seem to believe the child was real, but when he woke me later with the hungry baby squalling in his arms, the reality set in.

Hank soon fell asleep like a gangly colt, and Julian climbed into our bed and held us both. I looked in his beautiful face and saw conflicting feelings in his eyes.

"Julian," I whispered, hesitating. I had to tell him something, but it had to be said just right. "Do you remember Cheryl, who was here with Carla a few years ago?"

"Yeah … the redhead."

"Right. Well, after she had her daughter, she dropped everything—riding, painting, singing in the community choir. We all kept asking her if something was wrong with her or the baby. I remember this so clearly, but I couldn't understand it. She said, *After you have a child, all your love will be for her. Nothing else will matter. You'll never feel such passion again for a man.*"

Julian lifted his head up and leaned on one arm, gazing at me intently.

"Now I know … it's not true. Hank is our special creation. I love him dearly. But Julian … all my passion is still for you. I could live without the child. I could not live without you."

He put his lips on mine, as if he didn't need to hear another word. Little Hank slumbered on, unaware of the profound bond his parents shared that had nothing to do with him. Someday he would have these feelings for someone, and Julian and I would let him go into the world, but we would never let each other go or love each other less, even for the sake of the child. We both kissed the boy, as if acknowledging a sudden guilt. Of course, we loved him, but we had a secret joy in loving each other more.

You could never say the child wasn't spoiled. Everyone made such a fuss over him, promising him puppies and ponies and his grandfather's silver spurs (this from Julian). Marta made me eat properly so I'd have the best milk for Hank, and Askay would rock him to sleep when he was restless.

I enjoyed those early days with Robert Henry, watching him grow and change, laugh and cry, figure things out, run his toy truck and horse trailer all over the furniture. But often I looked out at the boys in the arena or Angie in the round pen with a scared horse or Julian on the grey (still sound) leading guests toward the green hills of summer. Marta noticed this and would take the boy in the late afternoon so I could walk out to meet the riders coming in from the trail.

When I saw Julian, my throat closed up, this many years later, at the way he sat his horse, straight-backed and deep in the saddle, hands light on the reins, legs relaxed and steady, balanced like no one I had ever seen. He never went right to the barn. He always loped over to where I waited and leaned down to kiss me, dust and sweat mingled with the taste of him that plunged deep into my being.

"Boy, I missed you today," he said once after an especially long ride. "The dudes were having a hard time, and lunch was late, so everyone was touchy. I started to get a headache, but I'm so happy these days, it didn't amount to much. The thing I needed the most was your arms around me."

"That can be arranged," I said.

"Hold that thought," he said and wheeled away toward the grey's stall.

Hank began sleeping through the night, and Julian and I made love as though it was the first time, finding new pleasure in familiar moves and playing that CD of "Almost Paradise" till it was worn thin, dancing in our darkened room, aching in a tight embrace and wishing for a hundred ways to say *I love you*.

Hank took his first steps a year later. I had been riding for several weeks, polishing Cielo's moves and reveling with the Nevada wind in my hair and sun on my skin. Hank was gripping the rail where he had crawled to watch me, and suddenly he slipped under the fence, stood up, and walked right over to the horse. I screeched, and he plopped down and started to cry.

"No, baby, oh no, you're a good boy!" I laughed and shouted for Julian, who had gone to the barn to meet the farrier.

He rushed back with alarm and saw Hank on the ground in the middle of the arena.

"How in hell … did he get out there?"

"He walked!" I answered.

Julian swooped him up and hugged him and then set him down again.

"Show Daddy, Hank!"

But the boy refused to move. We both sat on the ground with him and treasured the moment. It wouldn't be long until we couldn't keep up with him, and poor Askay was run ragged when I went out with

Julian and the wranglers on a trail loop. I usually turned around at the halfway point and rode back alone, sometimes trading horses with a guest who couldn't handle his mount that day, sometimes loping back over the hoof-trodden, smooth trails, enjoying the silence and the kaleidoscope of colors worthy of Helen's brush.

Sometimes I thought of Miranda. I had kept my promise over the years to visit her at the White Pine mental facility. I took her small gifts and let her talk about whatever she needed to. Some newer meds had helped her over the rough spots, but always, before I left, we would stand together and look at Helen's painting.

One time Miranda said, "I have come to know that hand so well. I have come to believe in love, even though part of me resides in that bronc."

"You've healed a lot, Miranda, and I'm glad."

"Has Julian?" she dared to ask.

"To be honest, no." But then I said to her, "I'm carrying his child."

"Oh, Serena, oh how wonderful. I hope it helps him. Really I do."

"In a few months, I won't be able to come as often."

"I know … but will you let me see the baby, if only once?" she asked.

"I can't promise that, Miranda, but I won't say *no* just yet. Can you wait on that?"

"Sure. I'm not going anyplace," she said with some sad irony in her voice.

I had wished then that Julian could see *this* Miranda. I thought he'd never forgive her, that he would hurt forever because of her crime, but at least he would see she was no longer a threat. Her treatment facility was much closer than Julian would have been comfortable with, but he never asked about it, and he never knew for sure if I was going to visit Miranda or Carla, going shopping or horse-hunting. It was better that way.

Now Hank was a year old, and I had not been to White Pine since his birth. I had talked to Miranda on the phone, and she seemed to accept my excuses, mostly involving Robert Henry, but now I was considering taking Hank with me to meet her. But this I wouldn't do without Julian's knowledge.

So that night, I tried to ask him. It wasn't easy. He'd had a tough day, having to lead a lame horse almost eight miles, and then, one of his greyhounds had died while he was gone.

"I don't suppose you need any more trouble today," I said, rubbing the knots out of his shoulders.

"Well, it might as well come all at once," he said with a sigh.

"I need to ask you something, and I already know what your answer will be," I said.

"Will I love you less for asking?"

"You might."

"Serena."

"Miranda wants to see Hank."

He looked at me like I'd hit him.

"Oh God, Julian, I'm sorry. I should never have asked you that."

"Would you have done it without asking?" he asked, still shaken.

"Absolutely not. I don't want to do it. I feel trapped in the round pen, Julian. Miranda is better, but I'm still holding the rope. I just keep hoping one more release on my part, and I can let her go. I haven't seen her for a year. She's taking her meds, going to counseling. I already told her *no*. I thought a *yes* might drive out all her demons."

"Not with our son, Serena. Please."

"I won't do it, Julian. It was a bad idea."

"I wish I had your heart, Serena, but I don't," he said, recovering a little from the shock. "But there is something I will agree to. When Hank is old enough to understand and finds out about Miranda, I won't stop him from seeing her. It has to be his choice." He looked at me with compassion. "When I first saw you in the round pen, I would have given you anything. I still will." He seemed to be struggling with his words, but he went on. "But our son is untouched by the things we know. I only want to shelter him as long as I can."

"I know, Julian, and I'm going to let you do just that. I'm glad you said *no*, really."

He took my hands. "I should be glad you trusted me enough to ask that question. I should never let you down with my fears."

"But I love your heart, whatever is in it," I said, and I placed my hand there, trying to slow its pounding.

"Serena, I'll go tell Miranda myself."

And he did. A few days later, I had to reveal where she was and watch him drive away from the ranch. I held little Hank in my arms and kept my eyes on the road until the truck was out of sight. I had never loved him more.

That evening after I put Hank to bed, I sat on the front porch and tried to name all the colors in the Nevada sunset. They were the colors of our lives, our horses, our dreams, no one better or brighter than the other, all blended to make a whole that had no name.

Julian pulled in and climbed wearily out of the truck. He sat down beside me on the swing and hugged me with one arm. He didn't say anything for a minute, almost as if he didn't know how to begin, and then, "Serena, you've worked a miracle with that woman. It was almost bearable. Miranda was beside herself to see me, but she didn't touch me or make any threats. She let me explain about Hank and only said, *Someday I'll save him for you.* That could be a fantasy, but it gave her hope that she could earn my forgiveness, so I let it go. She said, *Tell Serena I love her.* Damn if that didn't kill me, but she was so calm and dignified. I'm glad I went. I told her Hank could meet her on his terms, that I wouldn't stop him. She said, *I'll never hurt you again, Julian,* and I said, *I believe you.*"

We followed the fading purple and crimson and gold with our eyes until darkness filled the horizon, and then we went in to our son.

2

When Robert Henry was four, he pulled himself up on an old pony someone had left bridled and headed out into the desert after his father. Julian had been gone about ten minutes. I was riding Cielo, still going strong at age nineteen, but he wasn't a trail horse. I called up to the barn, "Clint, do you have a horse saddled?"

"Yes, ma'am."

"Could you bring him to me and put Cielo away? My child just ran away from home!"

Clint trotted down to the arena with a dun gelding, chuckling. "He won't get far, ma'am."

The pony had gone about a mile when he planted his feet and refused to take another step. Hank was kicking and crying to no avail. I rode up beside him.

"Trouble, partner?"

"This horse won't go!" He resumed wailing.

"Hank, Hank, stop that crying."

He looked at me stubbornly but staunched his tears.

"Okay, now give me your hand. You can sit up here with me, and we'll go find your father."

"What about Stormy?"

"I'll take the bridle off, and he'll go back to the ranch. Now come on."

I swung him into the saddle. He still fit in front of me. I handed him the reins and nudged the dun into a lope. It wasn't long before we caught Julian's guests where he had stopped to point out some geologic features.

"Looks like we have company, folks," Julian said.

I pulled in next to my husband. "Your son was coming after you on Stormy."

"Aha, you little bandit! Did you trick Mommy into bringing you out here?" Julian teased.

"No! Mommy tricked me!"

"Mommy tricked you?"

"Yes! She told me to stop crying. So I did. Then she made me gallop on her horse all the way out here!"

Guests were falling off their horses laughing. Robert Henry did not think it was so funny.

"I'm tired, and I'm thirsty," Hank complained.

"Well, I think we can fix that." Julian handed his son a canteen with Marta's sweet lemonade, and the boy guzzled it down.

Thunder rolled in the distance.

"We may have to cut this ride short. Serena, do you feel up to giving some lessons in the indoor arena?"

"Sure."

"I'll take Hank, and we can have a little talk on the way back."

"Good," I said, "but I'll bet you'll have the harder lesson to teach."

"No doubt about that, my love," Julian said. He grabbed Hank and kissed me all in the same move.

The first drops of rain fell as the ranch house came into sight. Four or five people headed for the arena, and Julian took Hank to the barn. I hoped he'd tell him the rattlesnake story, but I knew Julian didn't want to scare him. The child was impetuous, stubborn, and smart. He looked more and more like his dad, and I knew some day he'd be a heartbreaker, if someone didn't break his heart first.

After about half an hour, the rain and thunder was so loud the clients couldn't hear me, so we called it a day. Most of them were getting canter departs and correct leads, and some were asking for counter-canters. Others were happy with leg-yields and halts without using their hands. It was a good afternoon all around.

And it was a Saturday. We had missed very few over the years, and though Alberto had found a better job and had left us, Tyrone still sang "Almost Paradise," and Angie was trying to learn the duet with him. The guests always enjoyed that moment when Julian reached for my hand. I still felt the sensuality of his embrace, his thin hard belly against mine, and his sweet breath in my ear. We had been together almost ten years, but it always felt like the first dance.

At dinner, Julian had related his talk with Hank. The boy worshipped his father, so I know he listened. "I told him about the rattlesnake," Julian said.

I gasped.

"I told him I got very sick, and Mommy had to save me like Mommy saved him today. Then I asked what he would do if Mommy wasn't close by. He thought for a long minute. *I should watch out for rattlesnakes and don't go farther than Mommy can see.* I hugged him so hard and made him promise to follow that rule, a rule he had created himself. He nodded his wise little four-year-old head and promised on his piece of obsidian," Julian concluded.

"Oh dear, a black talisman," I said.

"Just his tie to earth, my dear. You have a black horse," he reminded me gently.

"Some black things have a light inside," I said.

"Are you a poet or a horsewoman?"

"I am the absolutely crazy fan of my boss, Mr. Julian Rose," I said, punching him lightly.

He held me at arm's length. "I'm saving myself for the dance," he said.

Later, I let him crush me against him and felt that familiar electric rush. Billy hadn't outgrown his fascination with our passion, though he now brought a girlfriend on Saturday nights, and she waited patiently for him to hold her like that. But we knew what it was that stayed his heart. We were his talisman, a thing he didn't want to touch too soon for fear it might break. One by one, the girls gave up and didn't come back.

"I'm looking for my *Serena*," he told Julian once, "and I'll know when I find her, just like you did, Mr. Rose."

3

Robert Henry resisted lessons, but by the time he was six, he could work in the round pen. He dressed every morning like his dad—jeans, white shirt, sometimes chaps, always blunt spurs. He was learning rope tricks and how to ride with a loose rein or no rein on his 14.2 hand Appaloosa mare, Sparkle. He needed very little help from us.

But that year, he started school, and his fairly undisciplined, free ranch life came to an end. The subtleties of elementary school rules were lost on him. He understood the need for rules, but they had to make sense or he was outraged. One time, his teacher called me to the kindergarten room where he'd been held after class. He sat at his desk in a quandary. "Miss Applegate wants me to color the lion in this picture before I can go home," he explained to me. "But I left it blank because I want it to be a *white* lion like the one Askay saw in Africa!"

"Rules are rules," Miss Applegate said. "All animals filled in."

"It's a stupid rule," Hank piped up.

"I have to agree, Miss Applegate," I said a bit more calmly. "His lions are white, which is perfectly acceptable to the actual white lions of South Africa. Perhaps he could bring you a picture of one tomorrow from one of his books?" I suggested.

She sighed. "I suppose this one time, but Henry has to follow procedure."

"He's six years old. Why are we stifling his creative spirit so early?"

That she couldn't answer, and we left with a smug smile on Hank's face.

When we got in the truck, I said, "You know, my boy, sometimes it's easier to follow the *silly* rules and save your energy to break the really *bad* rules."

"Like what?" he wanted to know.

"Like if you were ever told that there was a rule that black kids or Native American kids couldn't play with white kids. You should break that rule instantly."

"I don't know any black kids, but there are lots of Indians at my school," he informed me proudly.

"I want you to bring one of them home to ride with you. They are superb riders and could teach you something while you show others which rules to break."

"I'll do it!" he responded eagerly. "What does *superb* mean?"

"Very, very excellent."

"Dad's taking me to the Indian Races at the fairgrounds this weekend. I'm going to ask the winner if he'll be my friend!"

Literal, naïve Hank. I realized those boys probably hated whites getting in their business. I might have gone too far. I'd see how it played out. Very few people could resist Robert Henry Rose.

The day of the races, Hank was jumpy as a cat. "I'm going to break the rules!" he said to his dad as we climbed in the truck.

"It better be a stupid rule," Julian said.

"The worst!" little Hank replied.

Julian gave me a questioning look over the top of Hank's head.

I mouthed the words *I'll tell you later* as we bumped along the ice-heaved road toward the older part of town.

The fairgrounds were crowded and noisy. You could smell alcohol and animals, soiled straw and cotton candy. Julian headed toward the livestock barn and said he'd meet us at the track later. Hank could not even be lured to the Ferris wheel. He kept tugging me toward the dirt oval where the horses were warming up.

"Where are the Indians?" Hank cried.

"Robert Henry, I think they prefer to be called Native Americans," I told him.

"Okay." He paused, his young brain calculating. "Then what am I?"

"I guess you're a native American too, but your skin is a different color. Come on, child. I can't explain the history of the world in five minutes."

"Miss Applegate says Indians … um, Native Americans, killed lots of white settlers and cowboys."

"I think the killing went both ways, son. The point is there's no need for fighting anymore. There *is* a need for friendship."

"That's why *I'm* here," he said confidently.

"That's right."

"Oh, look, there's Miss Applegate! Wait till she sees what I'm going to do!"

Oh, Lord, I thought, *give me strength.*

We watched a few races.

"There are no Indians riding, I mean Native Americans," Hank wailed.

"Honey, it's a white boy's world," I said, but I don't think he heard me.

Then in the grassy center of the track, some wild-looking, rangy horses appeared. There were Appaloosas, pintos, pale palominos, and mustangs. Few of them were saddled, and some of the bridles consisted of merely a loop of thin rope in their mouths. The boys beside them were all ages, dressed in jeans and rag-tag shirts with tribal feathers hanging from their belts or beaded headbands holding back their dark, uncut hair. They were whooping and challenging each other in Native tongues. These were tough boys, sullen and fierce, and my six-year-old wanted to be right in the middle of them.

There were no rules for this race, ironically enough. Someone held the unruly mounts while the boys raced to jump astride them and take off. Nobody monitored shoving or kicking or blocking another's horse. It was each rider for himself, no stately entrance of thoroughbreds with jockeys in silks of their farm colors, saddles and bridles of polished leather, and expensive snaffles fit perfectly in purebred mouths. I suddenly wished Hank was sixteen, a foot taller, and street-hardened. I thought I had set for him an unreasonable task.

But he was not dismayed. He picked out a handsome, lean youth with a piebald stallion to root for, and when they announced the riders' names, his was Henry Dancing Horse. Hank cried, "Mommy! Mommy! He's the one! He's going to be my friend!"

The boy looked to be about fifteen. Eagle feathers hung from a narrow collar around his neck. He was lightly muscled and straight-limbed. He glanced haughtily across the field and gave a signal to his handler, who moved the stallion to the inside of the track. The kids lined up behind a chalk mark, and a gunshot rang out.

Three horses leaped out of the assistants' hands and barreled down the track. Henry Dancing Horse was the first to swing up on his piebald, and to my great surprise, he grabbed the hand of another boy, chased down one of the runaway horses, and let the boy recapture his mount with a flying swing! *Now that's friendship,* I thought. Just then Julian joined us but had missed the gallant act.

"We're rooting for Henry, on the piebald!" Hank screamed.

"His name is *Henry*?" Julian asked with disbelief.

"Henry Dancing Horse," I said with a sly smile.

And there he was at the front of the pack, two lengths ahead of the next horse, which the rider was having trouble staying on.

"Oh my God, this is crazy," Julian was saying.

Little Hank was stamping his feet and hammering the rail with his fists, crying, "Henry! Henry!"

There were bodies on the track, loose horses going the wrong way, and general mayhem. I had to close my eyes. Henry Dancing Horse won easily and pranced around on the turf, hugging his stallion and slapping the backs of the losers. People were helping the injured riders and catching the riderless horses. Hank slipped under the rail and ran toward the crowd of Native Americans.

Julian called out, "Robert Henry, come back here!" My husband turned to me. "He's not going out there!"

"Julian, stay here. I'll go," I pleaded. A white woman would not be the target Hank's father would be.

I stayed close behind my son, but not so close as to impede his cause. He walked right up to Henry Dancing Horse, stuck out his hand, and said," I knew you'd win! I knew it! Will you be my friend?"

The dark-skinned horseman looked down at the small white boy and flung away several arms that tried to knock Hank to the ground.

"What's your name, little boy?" the winner asked.

"Robert Henry Askay Rose," Hank said happily.

"Henry ... Henry Four Names. Did you cheer for me?"

"Yup."

"Did your parents let you come out here?"

"They sent me."

"Why?"

"To be your friend."

"I have lots of friends ... *Indian* friends," Henry Dancing Horse said.

"I don't see any white friends," Hank observed.

"I don't need any *white* friends," the arrogant boy replied.

"Okay ... but I need a Native American friend," Hank said simply.

That did it. The brown youth raised his arm and said, "Henry Four Names, give me your hand. I'll be your friend."

Then the other boys joined in, shouting, "Henry Four Names! Henry Four Names!" and someone put a necklace of crow and hawk feathers around his neck. Then big Henry lifted little Henry up on the lathered stallion and came my way.

"Ma'am," big Henry said, "are you this one's mother?"

"I am."

"I sure could use some help cleanin' up my horse. Could Henry go to the barn with me?"

"He's good with horses," I said, "but don't let him get in the way."

"You can have him back in an hour. I 'ppreciate it."

"Mom has a horse called Dancing Sky," Hank announced.

"Really," Henry said.

"He's all black and *big*, so big," Hank was explaining as they led the piebald away.

Julian put his arm around me. "I couldn't stay up there. I thought there'd be some trouble."

"The boys handled it just fine," I said.

Then Miss Applegate rushed over. "What are you doing letting Henry go off with those ruffians?"

"I'm letting him break some rules, Miss Applegate."

"I've heard about stuff that's gone on out at your place. Apparently, *rules* don't apply there," she huffed.

Julian just couldn't stand any more. "Miss Applegate, with all due respect, you don't know what the hell you're talking about!"

"I know what I know," she said, not giving an inch.

"Here's something you don't know. We'll not have our child taught to be a racist. If he wants a Native American friend or any other friend who's a different color or religion or lifestyle or whatever, we'll welcome those friends. It wouldn't hurt you to grow up a little and see the world through someone else's eyes. Everyone has pain. We can help each other or fight the bitter fight with our neighbors till there's nothing left to fight over, but our child is not going to be one of the mean-spirited bigots of the world."

"Well, I just hope those Indians don't hurt him. Henry's one of my favorites."

With that, Hank's teacher faded into the crowd, and Julian and I sat down on the grass, locking hands and checking our emotions.

"Nobody said this was going to be easy," Julian sighed.

"I'm so proud of Hank," I said. "And I really like that Henry Dancing Horse. Maybe he'll be like a big brother to our son."

"Well, we'll see how it goes. That young man may not always want a white-skinned tagalong. By the way, you look beautiful today," he added, "a tan glow on your face, and your eyes as blue as summer skies."

"Oh, you're a *cowboy poet* now?" I teased.

"When I'm with you."

"Is it our anniversary or something?"

"Every day is our anniversary, my dear Serena."

"I love you, Julian Rose."

We were just about to go after our boy when there was Henry Dancing Horse striding across the field with his hand in Hank's. It was a stunning sight. Even folks wandering in the grandstand stopped to watch. *The end of racism may take these small steps,* I thought. Julian got up and clasped big Henry's hand. "Thank you for taking care of my son," he said.

Dancing Horse looked Julian in the eye. "Mr. Rose, sir, you have a great kid."

Little Henry beamed.

"I'm happy to call him my friend," the older boy continued.

"Henry Dancing Horse, if you ever need a job, come to me first," Julian offered.

"Well, sir, I've only heard good things about your outfit. I'd love to work for you. But I have a couple more years of high school, and my folks need me on the res."

"Can you come out on a weekend, just to ride with Hank?" Julian suggested.

"Henry Four Names, how does that sound?" big Henry asked.

"Yes, yes, oh please come. You have to see my mom's black horse!"

The too-mature-for-a-fifteen-year-old looked at me then and said, "Dancing Sky. I like that."

"Well, he's a dressage horse, but you could probably make him whatever you wanted."

"Oh, no, ma'am, I wouldn't presume to do that. None of my horses go *on the bit*," he said, laughing.

"Let me guess. You read a lot," I said.

"Yes, ma'am. Can't get enough horses or enough books."

I squeezed his shoulder in approval. He glanced up at the stands and said, "I think we've caused quite a stir."

"It's called *progress*," I said, smiling.

"Took awhile, didn't it," he said.

"Way too long, son," Julian added.

"Can I stay with Dancing Horse longer?" Hank pleaded.

"I think it's time to go home, Hank, but your new friend can come to the ranch anytime." He turned to big Henry. "You know where we are?"

"Yes, sir. Everyone knows Rancho Cielo Azul," he answered. "Maybe I'll see you in a few days, Henry Four Names."

"Please," Hank responded.

Dancing Horse grinned and released Hank's hand. We parted and crossed the track before the next event. Trotters and sulkies were lining up for their races. We grabbed some tacos and headed for the parking lot.

"This has been the best day of my life!" Hank declared.

It was the line a parent longs to hear.

4

That's how Henry Dancing Horse came into our lives. Hank showed him all the special places on the ranch. The Native American showed Hank how to draw an arrow and hit a target, how to make his own beaded headband from chips of obsidian and rose quartz. I overheard big Henry asking Hank why he chose obsidian for a talisman. "I don't know. Maybe because when I first found one, I thought it was a big, black tear right there on the ground."

Henry Dancing Horse grabbed his heart with one hand and little Hank's shoulder with the other. "Henry Four Names, I'm going to tell you a true story. Many, many years ago on another desert south of here, there lived some fierce tribes of Indians."

"Native Americans," Hank corrected him.

"Well, anyway, these Native people were greatly feared by settlers, so they called in some soldiers, US Army Indian fighters, to chase them out of the land. The Native men left their women and children behind and galloped off on their best horses to lure the white men away. They ran and ran, but the soldiers had well-fed, strong animals, and they came closer and closer. The Indians—"

"What were they called?" Hank broke in.

"Apaches. The Apaches had no place to go. Their horses were getting tired, and it was late in the day. Here's the part of the story that no one knows for sure how to tell. Did the Apaches not see the huge cliff in front of them? Or did they race over it and die so they would never be captured by the soldiers?"

"Does this have a happy ending?" Hank wanted to know.

"You decide, Henry Four Names," Dancing Horse said. "The next day, all the women and children walked to the base of the cliff where their chiefs and fathers and brothers and sons had died, and they cried for three days. A million tears were shed on the lonely sandstone. Years after that, geologists and hikers and tourists dug into that cliff, and out fell hundreds and hundreds of pieces of black obsidian, just like yours. And the white people said, *These must be the Apache tears from that terrible day.*"

Hank threw his arms around Henry Dancing Horse, and between his sobs, he said, "I will never, never do anything to make your people cry!"

"I believe you, Henry Four Names. You see how special your talisman is? And you knew it was a tear. You knew it was a tear …"

Later, Hank told me the story and holding out his obsidian said, "Mommy, did you know this used to be a real tear?"

"What could be better for a talisman than a thing with two essences?" I answered.

"What is *essences*?"

"A thing's nature. Your obsidian is both volcanic glass and Apache tear."

Of course, when he tried to use that story for *show and tell*, his first-grade teacher said it was just a myth. No reasonable person would believe that. Hank was crushed. I assured him that just because some people didn't believe it didn't mean it wasn't true. He breathed a sigh of relief and kept that tear in his pocket for many years to come.

5

Henry Dancing Horse spent a lot of time on the ranch. Julian tutored him in accounting, the only subject that was keeping him off the Honor Roll at school. When they had plumbing problems on the reservation, I washed his clothes and gave him one of the guest cabins so he could shower. Big Henry taught Hank the secret of riding bareback and got a few of the wranglers to take part in *pretend* Indian Races, which they mostly let Hank win. Looking back, it was probably one of the least stressful spans of our lives.

The kids at the elementary school were awed by Hank's friendship with a Native American. He was chosen first for sports' teams and invited to birthday parties and camp-outs. Parents of his classmates would call and thank us for raising such a polite child. Hank informed us he was learning the Native American *rules* for life, first of which was to respect your elders.

"What's an *elder* exactly?" he asked.

"People like your dad and me!" I answered as quickly as I could.

One day, Dancing Horse came to the indoor arena where I was riding Cielo. He didn't say anything for a long time, and then when I halted next to him, he asked, "That's the horse with my name?"

"Yes, it is."

He stroked the black neck. "Could I try that?"

"I thought you'd never ask," I said. I jumped to the ground and handed him the reins.

"I mean bareback."

"Okay. You'll have to be quiet with your legs. He's very sensitive," I warned him.

"I'll be careful. I just want to do that dancing move."

"The *passage*?"

"That suspended trot," he said.

I gave him a little instruction, but he understood the feel of the horse, when he was balanced, when he was ready. He smiled over at me and lifted Cielo into his supreme dancing gait. Henry's seat did not falter. I had to remind him to keep his hands low and soft, but he was a pliant rider and allowed the horse to feel free between his legs and hands.

"Three twenty-meter circles and then give him a break," I called out.

"Yes, ma'am!"

He finished the routine and guided the black to the rail.

"Mrs. Rose, this is really asking a lot, so just say no if you can't do it. I have a dream of expressing my name in a real way for my people. They think I dance with all my horses, but it's not true. *This* horse really knows how to dance. If I could show him at the fair this year in the specialty event, I would make my Nation proud."

"I think it's a great idea, Henry. I can make up a choreography of his best moves, teach you how to do them, maybe find some music that fits. Yes! Drums and flutes, something from your Native American tradition written for Cielo's natural cadence! We'll wow them. Let's do it!"

"Oh, thank you, Mrs. Rose. I hope I can do right by the horse."

"He's pretty easy to handle. A few figures are difficult, but we'll work out a dance that suits you both. I'm excited about this, Henry," I told him.

But Hank was jealous of the time big Henry spent with Cielo. "Why did you get him started in that ol' *dressage* stuff," he asked one day.

"Hank, he came to me. He wants to prove his name to his tribe. You could help him."

"I could?"

"Sure. You could groom Cielo and learn how to braid his mane and maybe even do a part in the music."

"There'll be music?" he asked, his interest provoked.

"Yes. It's a *dance*. He'll need drums, flutes, and maybe rattles. He's going to ride in the specialty class at the fair next year!"

"Oh … that's a big deal," Hank admitted.

"Yes, it is."

"And you're letting him use Cielo. That's a big deal too."

I hugged him and sent him out to the arena with renewed hope in his vision of their friendship.

The next time I saw Henry Dancing Horse on Cielo Bailando, I was speechless. He was cantering in a ten-meter circle with only a soft rope in the horse's mouth, which looped back to Henry's hands. Cielo's neck was round, his face perfectly vertical to the ground. There was no tension in the movement. Out of the circle, Henry broke to the trot down the rail, then turned down the center of the arena and came toward me in a half-pass right. I had just taught him that last week with Cielo in a *double bridle*. Now he was doing it with a piece of rope instead of *two* bits!

He halted in front of me and said, "What do you think?"

"I think you're going to get a standing ovation during which you'll wish you had the bridle on!"

"Oh, I've already thought of that," he said, and he showed me how quickly the rope could be converted into a halter for more control over an excited horse.

"How long have you been riding him like that?"

"Only about a week. I usually start in the bridle, then do the exact same movements with the rope. Today is the first day I only used the rope."

"Well, it's an amazing thing, Henry," I said.

"He's an amazing horse, Mrs. Rose."

I decided not to tell Julian and let him be among the surprised spectators in the grandstand. Two ancient traditions would become one in the dance of a Native American on a European warmblood.

Later that summer, after Henry and I had designed his moves and transitions, he brought a drummer and a flute player from the reservation. John Talks-with-Ravens watched the boy and the horse for a while and then began pounding his deep bass deerskin-stretched-over-pine drum as Cielo's hooves hit the ground, a two-beat rhythm for the trot sequences. Little Henry shook the softer rattles, one in each hand, alternately one-two-three, one-two-three, when the horse cantered. Above it all, the flute sang a plaintive melody written by the player, eighty-year-old Solomon Singing Waters. Cielo danced gaily to the sounds, mouthing the rope like a bit and swinging his big frame under Henry's balanced hips. It was all coming together.

Everyone at the ranch was affected by the music and the presence of Henry Dancing Horse and his friends. Guests were allowed to watch from a distance and mingle with the fellows from the reservation afterward. Many times, we all had dinner together outside around a blazing fire, and the musicians would begin to play again.

Julian said, "We need to hire Solomon and John on a regular basis. What a great way to bring two cultures together. I can't believe I didn't think of this years ago."

He drew me closer to him in the chilly, late summer air. We were back a ways from the fire, letting clients have the warmest places. "Having you by my side, looking up at the Nevada sky full of stars, listening to the music of our first Americans, is a balm for my soul."

"*You* are a balm for my soul," I said while our son hopped in a newly learned Indian dance around the campfire with his rabbit-bone rattles.

6

Fair day couldn't come soon enough for Hank. He would be painted with the colors of his name, Henry Four Names, and dressed in a loincloth and falcon feathers. He wanted these feathers because that Peregrine was so rare in Nevada, and he was a rare *white* Indian. The birds were endangered and protected, but Native Americans could use the feathers if found on the ground.

Hank started second grade and corrected his name at roll call to Henry Four Names. Of course, we got a call from the school. The principal himself, a Mr. Gregor, said, "Look, I know you folks have been mixing with the reservation people, but there's a limit."

I said, "I'll be happy to give you Henry's four names for your records." And I did. "But I would be grateful if you allow the boy to keep his Indian name. It means so much to him, and I believe it's a way to honor our Native Americans. We put up too many walls between people who are different from us, don't you think?"

He fumbled around for a minute before he said, "We probably do, Mrs. Rose, but I have to deal with the wall *builders* as well as those who tear walls down."

"So which one are you going to be, Mr. Gregor?"

"I'm going to be one who calls your son Henry Four Names," he said firmly.

"Thank you," I said, relieved. One less battle to fight for Robert Henry Askay Rose.

The fair opened on a bright fall day with a hint of winter in the air. We needed our jackets to sit in the shaded part of the grandstand. I waited for Julian in the front row while he helped everyone in the staging area for the Specialty Class. Julian groomed Cielo to a gleaming black, remembering not to put Show Sheen on his back where Henry would sit. The Native Americans, including our son, were painted and dressed, their hair braided, instruments tuned, and last-minute planning whispered in a huddle.

Julian made his way to me through the throng of fair-goers anxious to see the unusual acts promised on all the posters in town. "I didn't see Cielo's double bridle in the trailer," he said.

"Not to worry, my love."

"I would never have dreamed of this day," he said. "No matter what happens, I'm so proud of all of them."

"I'm scared to death," I said, but I needn't have been.

The class began. There were riders with dogs on ponies, an actual zorse (a rare breeding of horses and zebras) who did a nice stock horse pattern, a teenager who roped two calves and tied them up in under five seconds, and a few others that got the crowd laughing and clapping. And then it was time for Cielo.

First the drummer came out sounding the beat of the black's *passage*, an elevated trot that was his specialty. The flute player went to the left, Hank to the right with his rattles. The grandstand was hushed, people straining to hear the music, and then Cielo Bailando came down the center of the arena with his half-naked, dye-painted rider trailing eagle feathers from his headband and from strips of cloth glued down his long, brown arms, one hand on the narrow rope that slid through the horse's mouth. Other riders had performed bridleless, even taking jumps, but no one had looked like this.

Henry Dancing Horse barely moved as he shaped the warmblood into intricate patterns, circles that enlarged effortlessly, half-passes that made the viewers gasp at the way the horse's legs crossed laterally while traveling forward, exquisite transitions between gaits, extensions that became collections building toward perfect tempi changes (flying changes of lead every three strides, two strides, and finally one stride). The sound of the instruments faded and swelled with Cielo's dance, capturing the audience in its core.

Then Henry did something even I knew nothing about. At the far end of the ring, he halted Cielo, reached down and slipped the rope out of his mouth, dropping it on his neck and asking for a canter. As the horse moved down the center line, Henry spread his arms out in the air, the feathers trailing like wings, and the musicians edged in toward him. They all reached the heart of the arena together, stopped and turned to face the grandstand. With an invisible cue from Henry, Cielo Bailando went down on one knee, and the Native American stood up on his back and folded his wings.

Everyone went wild clapping and shouting. Henry immediately fashioned a halter out of the rope so he could lead Cielo safely away. The trophy went to the teen who had roped the two calves, but Cielo and his Native American team won a shiny gold ribbon that read Honorable Mention and the praise of all who saw them. I just hugged Henry Dancing Horse. I could hardly speak. Hank was jumping up and down crying, "We did it! We did it!" He leaped into his dad's arms, and Julian raved about his son's part in the act.

"Mrs. Rose," big Henry was saying, "that was the best thing I've ever done."

"No, Henry, the best thing was the day you told Hank you'd be his friend."

Old Solomon Singing Waters had tears streaming down his cheeks.

7

When Hank was eight and Dancing Horse was seventeen, we all went to the older boy's high school graduation. We were the only white guests there. However, strangely enough, the speaker was white. His words were translated into Dancing Horse's language.

He ended his address with, "You boys and girls that graduated have the best chance to make something of yourselves. Go out into the world with pride in your heritage, but don't depend on it as your *only* heritage. There is a place for you outside the reservation."

Oh, yeah, I thought. *Hollow words in the face of reality.*

We met Henry's family, ate sweet fry-bread, and were uplifted by the drums as they beat out a story only a few understood. Hank loved everything about the Native Americans. He whispered in my ear at one point, "Thanks for letting me break the rules, Mom."

"It was the nicest thing you ever did," I assured him.

"Miss Applegate didn't think so, but I told her she just didn't know what she was missing, not having a Native American friend."

"Good for you!" I said and thought, *That was almost two years ago, and he still remembers that teacher's fear of his friendship with Henry Dancing Horse.*

Julian and big Henry were talking about a job. "I could use two skilled horsemen right now. We have a full season ahead, and I seem to be getting tied up in the cattle business."

"My cousin is a hard worker and can trim a horse solid. Good with lameness too. I trust him."

"That's good enough for me," Julian said. "When can you start?"

"Mr. Rose, we can only work during the week. Our folks need us Saturdays and Sundays."

"Well, that will have to be okay then. We try to give everyone Monday off, but if you want to come out, there's always something to do, get you right on the payroll," Julian explained.

"We'll be there, sir. My cousin is called Frank Wandering Fox," Henry said.

"Be sure to tell Hank *that* story," Julian said.

Those boys turned out to be some of the best wranglers Julian had ever had. A couple of cowboys quit, saying they weren't comfortable with the Native Americans, and we hated to see that happen, thinking we had banished racism from our Rancho Cielo Azul. Angie and Frank hit it off from the beginning. Frank was quite a bit older than Henry but still younger than Angie, but it didn't seem to make any difference. They just looked at the world the same way and loved being together with the horses and out on the Nevada range doing a job. Billy started watching *them* dance on Saturday nights!

That year, Julian decided to build a permanent tent-camp up in a tree-lined draw about nine miles from the ranch. It was wild country bordered by Forest Service and pockets of wildlife sanctuaries. You could see range burros, antelope, coyotes, rattlesnakes, golden eagles and other raptors descending on jack rabbits and prairie voles, and an occasional mountain lion or bobcat. The draw had a spring and opened at the top to a lush meadow where the stars fairly fell to the horizon on a clear night. The elevation was 11,360 feet. It was not a place for everyone. The snow covered the land in winter and sometimes lingered in the shaded woods, even as guests began making the climb with their horses in late spring.

Clients had started coming earlier in the year and staying later, so popular was our English riding program, round pen training, and sensitive, well-broke horse string. Carla would come help me when she could. We still enjoyed each other's company. We'd go out on the trail after lessons, and I showed her the cliffs where Julian's parents died, the cabin where Julian was born, even the high tent-camp, where we waited one night for the full moon to be positioned in the sky for its light to guide us down.

We made a small campfire and ate some cold chicken and chocolate cake Marta had packed for us. The wind tossed the pine branches in a soft symphony with the waters of the spring creek. Carla looked beautiful in the firelight. She had been pretty quiet all afternoon and now started to say something and then stopped herself.

"What?" I said.

"I don't know. I guess I've just wanted to tell you for a long time that I think I made a mistake."

"How?"

"I let you go," she said.

"Oh, Carla, things worked out for the best."

"For you maybe. What you and Julian have … well, I'll never know that kind of love."

"Why not?"

"Because I still love you. I was afraid of it years ago, didn't understand it really. But no man has ever made me feel the way you did, or cared about me the way you did. I don't even like a man's hands on me." She paused and then asked, "What's it like … with Julian?"

"When Julian touches me, I feel like fainting. When you first touched me, I felt that way too. But when he pulls me against him in that dance to 'Almost Paradise,' it feels like a bolt of lightning drenches my soul. That I never felt with you. When Julian kisses me, I feel whole. When you kissed me, there was always something missing," I admitted.

"Yeah, me kissing you back!" she said.

"Maybe. The thing is, Carla, I loved you, but I'm not gay. When I look at Julian's face, his body, I think it's the most ravishing thing in the universe. I literally ache with the thought of him, and not just for the sex, but with the thought of his needs, his dreams, his ideas, with the way he sits a horse, the way he treats his wranglers and clients, the sound of his voice, his smile. Even sickness and tears pull me inside out with wanting him, loving him. I never had the chance to feel those things with you, Carla, but even if I had, and happened to meet Julian, I'm not sure I could have stayed with you. I hope it doesn't hurt you to hear this," I said.

"No, it just gives me regret. I'll never know for sure if I could have been all those things for you."

"Well, our friendship means a lot to me. I wouldn't want you anywhere but in my life—truly, Carla."

"Thanks, Serena. It helps to talk about it. I didn't want to keep that part of my heart from you."

"I thought about you so much when I first knew Julian. I thought I just had a rebound crush. But after all these years, I believe he is my true love, my only love."

"I'm glad for you, Serena, really I am. I just didn't know what was right in front of my eyes. That's life, I guess."

"There's someone for you, Carla. It will happen."

"I'm not getting any younger."

"But you know who you are now! You'll be more open to the love that was meant for you. We didn't know anything back then, just that being together felt good. That wasn't enough for the long haul."

The moon was high now and brilliant. We stamped out the fire, filling the pit with dirt, and bridled our horses. We could clearly see the trail and the white pines stretching up to the sky on either side, and then the rock outcroppings and cactus dotting the sparse landscape lower down.

"Sing that song for me," Carla said.

"*Almost paradise, we're knocking on heaven's door. How could we ask for more?*"

"You couldn't ask for more, Serena," Carla broke in. "You got heaven and then some."

When Hank turned ten, Julian and I had been married for fifteen years. That Christmas, we danced to "Almost Paradise" and spent a few days in the canyon. Marta took care of little Hank, who was not so little anymore—still a child, but tall for his age and oh so wise, half raised by a Native American, half raised by a Mexican and an African! What a lucky boy.

The honeymoon house was couched in snow and held such poignant memories. We sat in front of the fire, enjoying the warmth, the silence, and the many reminders of Helen and Henry. Julian made love to me like never before. I couldn't imagine a deeper pleasure. The years had barely touched Julian. He was as lean as Dancing Horse, his wonderful face unlined. His eyes had an extra softness when he looked at me, his hands an enrapturing grace. He didn't speak when he gathered me up, and I liked that. Words were not needed for what we gave to each other in the secluded night.

Before the New Year, we were back at the ranch. Hank had waited to open his Christmas presents, and Askay made us a Tanzanian meal. The months without guests were special. We could read or ski cross-country, groom horses in the heated barn, and play with the dogs. The Border collie and Sandy were both gone, one greyhound languished at fourteen, not even bothering to chase the cats. Hank wanted a dog, a German shepherd, and we told him when he was twelve, we'd consider it. He was doing well in school, and we didn't want another distraction for him. Dancing Horse was enough! The things those boys dreamed up! But we always felt Hank was safe with big Henry.

I drove out to see Miranda one day when Julian had a meeting in Winnemucca. I hadn't been there for a while, but she seemed to understand how busy I was with Hank, ranch projects, and more clients every year. She appeared lonely but didn't feel like talking. I described the scene at the fairgrounds, and she smiled at the thought of Julian's son with feathers around his neck, shaking his Native American rattles.

"When I meet him, it will be for a good purpose," she said.

It had been fifteen years since she was sentenced to White Pine. There was a smudged line on Helen's painting where Miranda's finger had rubbed a mark between the gift in Helen's hand and the scared horse.

"This belongs to someone else now. I just don't know who it is," she said sadly.

"Miranda, no one will take it from you," I promised.

"No … I'll give it freely … you can go now, Serena."

I touched her arm. "Are you all right?" I asked.

"I don't know. I don't feel angry. I don't feel anything."

Years of drugs, the same drab room, the same damaged inmates, and the same conversations had left her numb. I could never tell Julian this.

"I need to do one good thing in my life," she said suddenly.

"Miranda, you have. You gave up Julian. That was huge. I thank you every day for that, the way that you did that."

"Something greater, something consequential," she said.

"I hope you find out what that is." I rose to leave. "I hope it's your final healing."

"Thank you, Serena. I do love you, such as my love is," she said softly, and she turned away.

I drove slowly back to the ranch. Julian wouldn't be home until tomorrow. I could spend some time helping Hank with his homework and hear about the two Henrys' adventures. The word *dog* came up often in our conversations!

A few weeks after Hank's twelfth birthday, Henry Dancing Horse came up to the house when Hank was in school. He had a concerned look in his eyes. Julian was out on the range gathering steers with Carson and Clint.

"Henry? Is everything all right?" I asked. We sat down in the living room. He was very uncomfortable.

"Ma'am, there's something I need to tell you. Maybe it's my imagination, but I think you should know." He paused dramatically. "There's a girl at Hank's school that's bothering him."

"You mean bullying?"

"No … I mean … sort of flirting, trying to get his attention."

"Well, that's bound to happen. What worries you?"

"The girl is sixteen, almost seventeen. Some kids are afraid of her, Hank tells me, but he's not. He likes her. He started dressing up a little, showing off his muscles, talking tough. I told him to take it easy, she was trouble. But Hank, you know, doesn't like to be told what to do."

"Why would a seventeen-year-old be interested in a child?" I asked in true amazement.

"Well, he's as tall as she is and doesn't look or act his age. I think he's flattered. He says she's really pretty and, ah … sexy."

"Oh, God."

"She'll be graduating next year, if she doesn't drop out. She's practically failing now. Some teacher thought Hank should tutor her in English and Earth Science, he's so advanced in those subjects.

Hank would kill me for telling you. Maybe you can just be aware, keep him home at night, stuff like that. The girl has a car … I'm just saying …"

"Henry, I thank you with all my heart. You did the right thing."

"He's like my little brother. I don't want him to get hurt."

"You're a guardian angel, Henry," I said.

That night, I asked Julian to find a German shepherd for Hank. He gave me a curious look.

"There's a girl at school taking too much interest in him. He's not ready."

"I agree. Should I talk to him?"

"No. I promised big Henry I wouldn't say anything," I answered. "I think if Hank really likes this girl, we're in big trouble. She's seventeen and has a questionable reputation."

"Should we speak to his teachers?"

"We might. I don't want Hank to think we're checking up on him for something that may be purely innocent. But I'd like to know more about the girl."

"Yeah, so would I," Julian said.

Monday, I drove in to the local K–12 campus. This year, Hank had Daryl Pearson for homeroom, so I went there first during the teacher's free period. Hank was in Algebra. I didn't think he'd see me, and if he did, I'd say Mr. Pearson called me in. I was sure the teacher would go along with that.

"Mrs. Rose, how nice to see you," he said, getting up from his desk. "Are you here about Hank? He's doing fairly well. Grades have slipped a little since he joined the track team, but a boy should be well-rounded."

"Mr. Pearson, I'll get right to the point. I need to know about a girl in the junior class. It seems she has a crush on my son, and I'm concerned."

"A junior, you say? What's her name?"

"I don't know, Mr. Pearson. An older girl hanging around Hank. I hoped you might have seen something."

"I don't deal much with upper classmen, but maybe they're just friends or on the varsity team together. I hear Hank is quite good at cross-country."

"I don't think a seventeen-year-old girl should be *speaking* to a twelve-year-old boy, much less forming any kind of relationship," I pressed on.

"Well, I'll look into it, Mrs. Rose. I haven't noticed anything unusual," he said. He turned back to his paperwork.

Weeks went by. Julian brought home a gorgeous female puppy, a German shepherd of sound bloodlines, black and tan, with a haunting, intelligent face and sensitive demeanor. Hank named her Paraíso after the ranch and her perfect conformation. She was eight weeks old and needed care, training, and love, which Hank was eager to give. We relaxed our watch.

He never mentioned the girl, or any girl. He got totally wrapped up in his dog and running. He was home from practice by six, studied until nine or ten after dinner, and went to his room. He had his own telephone, but it seldom rang, and usually it was Henry Dancing Horse. But something didn't feel right. A twelve-year-old should not be running long distance, at least not with such compulsion. Hank kept extending his mileage—six, then ten, then fifteen miles. He talked about marathons and filled his book shelves with *Runner's World*.

He seemed to be racing *from* something, as far and as fast as he could, his only companion Paraíso, as soon as she turned seven months old. A boy and his dog. Comforting. But the alarms were going off. He would only eat salad and meat. Askay slipped in the carbs now and then, but those foods were often untouched on his plate, even though he knew they could help his energy and endurance.

Julian was so busy with guests and new horses and the Cattlemen's Association, he didn't notice when his boy became a man, when little Hank became Henry Four Names for real, running across the unforgiving desert, hard and fearless, the snake story forgotten, his cowboy heritage flailing in the wind behind him.

Henry Dancing Horse left us for a lovely Native girl and moved to Winnemucca. I heard him tell Hank, as they stood by Henry's truck saying good-bye, "Don't keep secrets from the ones who love you."

"I don't have any secrets," Hank said.

"You will." Henry grabbed the younger boy's strong shoulders. "Trust me."

Trust. The one thing Julian and I valued most in our own relationship.

10

A year passed. Dancing Horse returned with wife and child. They had hated city life and missed the open desert, the horses, the silence. We let them live in one of the larger guest cabins, and Henry went back to work for Julian.

"Hey, where's little Hank?" was the first thing Henry asked.

"He's at a cross-country meet, running the Devil's Pass marathon," I answered.

"Oh, man," Henry moaned. "Get me a horse. I need some sanity in my life."

Julian was so happy to have him back. He spent hours with him on the trail, maintaining new riding loops and repairing the high tent-camp that the last winter had nearly destroyed. I tried to get my husband to see the errant path our son was on, but he just kissed me and said, "You worry too much. At least he's not wanting to fly an airplane!"

Paraíso waited at the gate day and night for Hank to return. He'd pet the dog affectionately and throw her rawhide stick for her a few times, but then he'd stumble in to bed, saying he was *too tired for words* and had to run farther tomorrow to get ready for some race we'd never heard of. His grades slipped a little more. He never got on a horse and barely spoke to Henry. "He's got his family now. He doesn't need me," Hank said.

"But maybe you need him," I said.

"No … he'll just hold me back."

"Where are you in such a hurry to be, son?" I asked.

"In someone else's skin," he replied and closed his bedroom door.

One day, he decided he wanted more money than his allowance provided, and he asked us if he could breed Paraíso and sell the puppies.

"I don't mind you selling puppies, young man, but what will the money get you that you don't already have?" his father asked.

"You wouldn't understand."

"Try me," Julian said.

"I need some better clothes. My stuff's for babies."

"Robert Henry, you have the best ranch clothes money can buy."

"That's the point," Hank said. "I'm not a jeans and white shirt kind of guy."

"You used to be," his dad said.

"Things change."

By the time he was fourteen, that statement couldn't have been truer. He became moody and sullen. He rushed through his chores, cleaned up after Paraíso and her litters, and disappeared. We could hear him on his cell phone late into the night. When we made the rule *no calls after ten,* he put the phone down on the kitchen table and said, "That won't make any difference."

He struggled with Algebra but wouldn't ask for help. Teachers called and complained that Hank was rude and uncooperative. I thought of that moment Julian and I felt more passion for each other than for our son. Did we drive him from us, drive him out of the paradise we had created for ourselves? Or was there something drawing our child from the world that we thought was best for him?

It was a tough year. Winter descended like a vengeful god, and Julian kept coming in from the cold with a debilitating cough. He needed Hank to help gather cows and tend to the horses. Sometimes Julian just couldn't put in a full day's work. Hank seemed to resent the intrusion on his private landscape. Henry Dancing Horse did more than his share and even paid Hank to watch little Rachael

Endless Rain, Henry and Willow's precious girl who had been born during the longest days of rain ever recorded in Nevada.

Robert Henry consented to eat meals with us and didn't talk much about running. I tried to get him to ski with me, but he said it was boring. Paraíso kept me company until the snow got too deep. The school bus only came out as far as the ranch three days a week that winter. The roads were icy and drifted badly from the crossroads to town. Hank fell behind in most of his subjects. Marta saved his grade in Spanish, and Julian was able to get him interested in history, especially the role of Native Americans in our country's westward expansion. I made him read and write, and for a while, things felt normal.

During spring thaw, when Hank turned fifteen, he melted out of our lives like the highland snow under the burning sun. He started coming home late, even though track hadn't begun. Some older-looking boys dropped him off and sped away without so much as a backward glance. He ignored Paraíso's puppies but banked the money from them happily enough. More than once, he was caught driving off in one of Julian's old trucks, even though he only had a learner's permit, and coming back late, one time near midnight.

He had always confided in us, showing us his secret forts on the desert, admitting his disappointment in poor grades, his sheer joy at winning a distance race. This was different. He seemed afraid somehow to be the boy we knew he was.

One night, he called from the crossroads. He'd broken an axle on an ice heave in the road, hurrying to get home. It was 1:30 AM. Julian was furious, so I said maybe I ought to go for him.

"We'll both go. He's not getting a chance to put one of us against the other."

At the crossroads, Hank was subdued and apologetic, mumbling something about the bad roads and poor visibility.

"Where have you been?" his father demanded.

"Don't you care about the truck?" Hank asked.

"I can replace the truck. I can't replace my son!" Julian told him.

"Mom?"

"We need to know where you've been," I said, somewhat more calmly.

"I … met someone."

"Someone, who?" Julian asked.

"A girl."

"Just tonight?" Julian went on.

"No, a couple of months ago," Hank admitted.

My heart stopped. Could this be that same wild girl that Henry had told me about?

"And there's some reason you can only see her at night?" Julian was asking.

"Well, I have school and chores, and she has a job."

"She's not in school?" I asked.

"She graduated," Hank said.

"How old is this girl?" Julian's question hung in the air.

"What difference does that make?" Hank challenged his dad.

"Right now, not a bit, because you're coming home, and since tomorrow is Saturday, I might have a few things for you to do."

"I'm sorry about the truck," Hank said, trying to get back in his father's good graces.

"I know you are, son. I'm just glad you're not hurt."

"But you think my girlfriend will hurt me," Hank said defensively.

I felt the shiver go through Julian's body as I sat in the middle next to him, Hank on the passenger side. There was an uncomfortable silence. Then Julian reached over me and grasped his son's shoulder. "Robert Henry, there are things in this world you can't imagine. Your mother and I answered the question a long time ago, *How will we get through the bad times*, in the same breath—with trust. You'll have to trust me, son."

When we finally got to our room at three, Julian sat on the edge of the bed, some nameless despair in his eyes. I ran my hand across his back and tried to think of the right thing to say. There were so many ways this situation could go, none of them good. When he lay back beside me, he pressed one of my hands to his heart.

In the morning, Askay had made a wonderful African breakfast, porridge and mangoes and thin slices of calf liver grilled to perfection.

Julian ate a few bites and went over to his reading chair. I waited at the table for Hank. He came in disheveled, as if he had slept in his clothes. I started in easy on him.

"Hank, your father and I didn't know you were dating anyone. You haven't introduced us to anyone special at school or track meets. Isn't there a girl your age you'd like to see?"

"Girls my age suck!" he said vehemently.

"Watch your language, son," Julian said, peering over the top of the morning paper.

"All right. Girls my age are skinny, silly, and boring."

"Not *all* of them," I suggested.

"Okay. Mom, how old were you when you fell in love with Dad?"

"Thirty."

"I rest my case," he said, satisfied.

"Oh, God, she's not thirty!" Julian said.

"No … twenty."

"Heaven help us," his father said. "What else should we know?"

"She's beautiful, funny, sensitive … and she loves me," he answered.

"That's not exactly what I meant," Julian said. He put the paper down and came over to sit at the kitchen table. "Look, son, I'm not going to judge someone I've never met. Bring her out to the ranch."

"You mean it?"

"Sure. Does she ride?"

"She likes horses. She says they talk to her."

Julian and I glanced at each other.

Hank went on. "I thought Mom could give her some lessons."

"I'd be glad to," I said.

"What's her name?" Julian asked.

"Liana," Hank replied. "I can really bring her out here? That would be so cool."

"Your mother and I can be quite *cool* when necessary," Julian said.

"Hank, I want to know how long you've known this girl," I persisted.

He didn't answer right away but fidgeted a little.

"The truth, son," I said.

"Well … I've known her for three years, but we've only really dated for two months, like I said."

"Oh, now that you're all of fifteen, she thinks it's appropriate to date you! Hank, this is not a good idea," Julian insisted.

"But it's *my* idea," he replied.

"Are you sure?" I asked.

"What's that supposed to mean?" he responded with annoyance.

"A twenty-year-old surely has other interests," I suggested.

"She's always liked me," he said.

Julian shook his head. "My God, three years ago you were twelve!"

"I've never looked my age. She thought I was fifteen then!"

"I cannot wait to meet this perceptive woman," Julian said. He returned to his newspaper but had not begun to read yet, I noticed.

Hank was saying, "I'll bring Liana to the round pen tomorrow."

"All right, son. That's always a good place to start."

"You and I might have a different take on that," he said.

Yes, I thought, *I imagine we do.*

Hank went to his room to call Liana. Julian looked up at me. "I have a terrible feeling about this," he said.

I put a hand on his tan cheek. Just touching him gave me courage. We would always be all right.

11

The next morning, Liana showed up in a red Mustang, gunning the motor as she pulled toward the barn to meet Hank. I walked that way in her dust. *She couldn't stop at the house first?* I caught a glimpse of bright red hair flipping through the barn door. I heard them talking in excited tones as I got closer.

"You'll like her, I promise," Hank was saying.

"Yeah, but what if she doesn't like me?"

"She gets along with everybody," Hank said.

"She better," Liana said.

We'll see, I thought.

When I entered the hay-scented old barn, my son was kissing a lanky, stunning woman in white shorts and a low-cut tank top revealing very tan breasts. *She must sunbathe in the nude … or spend hours in a tanning booth.* After all, summer had barely begun. They broke apart quickly.

"Mom, this is Liana," Hank said.

"Hi, Liana. I'm Serena."

"Mrs. Rose," she said formally, without quite meeting my eyes.

"Please call me Serena. I hope you brought some long pants."

"No … am I riding today?"

"I had hoped you would," I said.

"I don't have a lot of time today. I go to work at three," she explained.

She was flamboyant but comely. In a way, she didn't really act like a twenty-year-old. She took no lead in the conversation and kept fussing with her hair. Her legs were nicely shaped but had a girlish look to them. She obviously had not been on the track team. She had hooked one finger through a loop on Hank's jeans, as if he were a prize she'd won at the fair.

"Would you like to see some of the horses at least?" I asked.

"Well, actually, I'm kind of afraid of them," she admitted.

"I'm pretty good at fixing *that* problem," I told her.

"But sometimes they talk to me," she said.

"What do they say?" I asked.

"Oh, things like, *Open that gate, I want out,* or *I'm going to buck you off!*"

"I don't believe horses think like that," I assured her.

"You callin' me a liar?" she countered with a challenging smile.

"Liana, I'm on your side, really. I'm not judging you. But honestly, I think you're too old for my son. That doesn't mean I think you're a liar or—"

"Or what? Crazy?"

This was getting out of hand. Hank gave her a pleading look. "No, I think no such thing. I only meant that from my experience, one can deal with horses without jumping to the conclusion they're out to get you."

"Show me one of your horses, and I'll tell you what he says!"

"Maybe on another day, Liana, when you get to know the horses better. This doesn't seem like the best time," I said reasonably and turned toward the open door.

I heard Hank say, "See, I told you she was cool."

"I think she's a control freak," Liana whispered, but I heard her and felt defeated. Julian would not be happy. I wondered how much I should tell him about this first visit.

When he came in off the range, I had my answer. He was ashen-faced and not sitting straight in the saddle. He struggled off the horse and handed the grey, whose side was slathered with mud, to Billy.

"What happened?" I asked, helping him stay on his feet.

"He fell on me … in a bog," Julian gasped with pain.

"I'm taking you to the hospital."

"No … no, Serena. I think I just cracked a couple of ribs. I'll be all right. Let me lie down for a while."

"Okay, love."

We walked slowly toward the house. Askay came running out and supported Julian on his good side. "Do you need powders for bruising, for pain?" he asked softly.

"I'm afraid so … not as tough as I used to be."

"Mr. Julian, I always have strength from *you*."

Askay was the best. His love was unconditional and complete. Here he was, away from his family, away from the verdant hills of Tanzania, giving us his very heart, his life, really. We had offered many times to send him to Africa to reconnect with his tribe, a son he had left years ago to work for the Roses, to be able to send that boy to university, but he always said, "*Asante sane* (thank you very much). I stay … with you."

We eased Julian onto the couch, and Askay went off for his drugs. I washed Julian's face and gently removed his torn shirt. His side was already purple with bruising.

"It's been that kind of day," I said, wiping some mud from his arm.

"Liana?"

"Could have gone better." I wanted to spare him the details.

"Is she still here?" he asked.

"No, had to go to work. Hank seemed pleased that I met her and kept my disapproval from showing too much. He's been out there grooming horses since she left and even tossed a stick for Paraíso."

"Tell me the worst thing," Julian said, reaching for my hand.

I sighed. "She was rude, suspicious. Hank saw it but just kept encouraging her to like me. He's definitely the more mature of the two. I'd think he'd be tired of her contrary nature by now, but she is beautiful, in a petulant, beauty-queen kind of way. I don't know, Julian. I'm baffled by the whole thing."

"I'm grateful I wasn't here," he said. "I'm just not ready for … surprises."

Askay came in and helped Julian sit up so he could swallow some tea steeped with African medicines. I went to the bedroom and got him a clean white shirt. He winced as I eased him into it.

"I'm so sorry you got hurt, Julian. You didn't need any more pain in your life."

"Well, I won't be a very good dance partner, will I?" He tried to laugh.

"You're what I need, dancing or not dancing," I whispered in his ear.

"Not dancing may be all you get for a while." He kissed my hand closest to his lips.

"God, how I love you," I said.

"Can you help Ty with the guests tomorrow? Maybe take Hank with you. I want him hooked on this ranch a few more years. You might be able to tell him that with more diplomacy than I could."

"I'll do what I can, Julian. You know I'll hate being away from you for one minute."

"I know. You are a salve for any wound."

I kissed him deeply, careful not to crush him in my arms. His vulnerability aroused me in startling ways. I put a light throw over him and propped his sore back against a couple of pillows. I noticed one side of his face was swollen.

"Do you want some ice for that?"

"Yeah, I guess," he answered. "I really just want you."

"Any time," I said, putting my hand on his bare chest where I'd left the fresh shirt open. "Will you be okay while I go check on the trail plans?"

"I'll try," he answered, relaxing some from Askay's remedies.

When I got to the barn, Hank was cleaning his father's saddle.

"Is Dad okay?"

"I think so … just bruised. How 'bout his horse?"

"Ty says all he needs is liniment. Dad kind of broke his fall, I guess," Hank said.

"I think we should build some bridges over those bogs. They get worse every year. Would you like that job?" I asked him.

"Sure. I'll help with that."

Thank you, God, I said to myself, and then to my son, "What's the plan for tomorrow?"

"Ty thinks the cliff loop will be the driest. There's eight clients signed up for the ten miles. But, Mom, can you go with Ty and Clint? I promised Liana I'd meet her before she went to work."

"I can go." I had vowed not to say anything about Liana, but Hank jumped right in.

"Mom, something funny happened after you left the barn this morning."

I waited for him to explain, anxiety rising in my heart.

"Paraíso growled at Liana. I made her try to pet her after she said, *That dog doesn't like me.* Was it my fault?" he asked.

"No, son, the dog's due to whelp, in what, three weeks?"

"Yeah … but she's never done that before."

"What did you do?"

"I yelled at Paraíso. I didn't want to hit her. She's such a good dog."

"What did Liana do?"

"This is the odd thing. She just kept saying over and over, *You should get rid of that dog.* We talked about other things, and then she said that again when she got in her car to leave. I don't know what to do, Mom."

"When Liana's here, put Paraíso in her kennel. There's no sense in provoking an accident."

"What did you think of Liana?"

"Oh, Hank, I can't answer that yet. She wasn't at her best. She was defensive and disrespectful. I wouldn't think you'd be drawn to someone like that."

"But I love her," Hank said.

"I understand you have feelings for her, but *love*? That's such a complicated thing."

"It doesn't seem complicated to me," he said.

"It can get complicated by … Hank, you can love someone and have that love compromised by issues of trust and … things you can't imagine."

"Did you and Dad have these *issues*?" he wanted to know.

"No, not with each other. We've been very lucky. There were outside things that could have destroyed us, but we faced them, giving everything in our hearts for *each other.* I would never have told your father to get rid of an animal he cared about or desired him for what *he* could give *me*."

"Maybe if Liana is around you and Dad for a while, she'll see things differently, not be so … selfish," Hank said hopefully.

"That could happen, son, but will you just take it slow, for me?"

"Okay, Mom," he said a bit soberly. "I'll get your horse ready in the morning so you can take care of Dad."

"I would really appreciate that, my boy," I said, thinking, *That's the Hank I know.*

I went back to the house. I could tell Julian about *this* conversation, maybe not the part about Liana asking Hank to get rid of Paraíso. That was just bizarre.

Julian woke up when I sat beside him on the couch.

"Feel better?" I asked.

"A little. Askay said I could have more remedies in about an hour. I'm watching the clock. How's my horse?"

"He's doing fine. Apparently, you got the worst of it. Hank cleaned your tack, and he's saddling my horse in the morning so I can be with you longer."

"Can't Hank take my place? It would be good for him."

"I know, but I told him he could go spend some time with Liana. I think he's already having second thoughts about that relationship."

"Really?"

"He says he loves her but can't understand why she wants him to get rid of Paraíso." I knew I couldn't keep that from my husband.

"What?"

"I guess the dog growled at her."

"Maybe we should listen to the dog," Julian said.

"My thought exactly, but I'm going to trust Hank. He needs to make the right choice for himself."

"Ever the round pen reasoner," Julian said, squeezing my thigh.

"Careful, cowboy," I said. "I don't think your cracked ribs can follow through!"

He tried to laugh but groaned instead. Some of the guests were coming in for dinner, so Julian limped over to the main table. He could barely stand but made a brave face. He apologized for not eating with them and promised them they'd enjoy the next day's ride with me. They wished him well and let him go on Askay's arm.

I stayed about twenty minutes, telling them about the place we were going, leaving out any word of the plane crash for now.

Sometimes Julian let the story be known, and other times he didn't even slow the horses down as they trod over the very ground where his parents had died. That night, I took Helen's painting off the wall and said, "We're going here." Everyone approved and started questioning Hank as he came in, and I slipped out of the conversation and the room.

Askay had helped Julian out of his clothes and into bed. He reached for me. "Did you tell me everything about Liana?" he asked.

"Maybe not quite *everything*," I admitted. I continued reluctantly, "I saw something in her eyes ... like Miranda's."

"God in heaven," Julian said.

"I could be wrong. Maybe she's just a scared twenty-year-old who doesn't do well with authority figures like her boyfriend's parents."

"But you think there's more to it."

"I do. But the only way to find out is to let her be Hank's girlfriend. It's risky, but if we separate them now, it will just drive them together."

"I don't think I can let him take that chance, Serena. My whole life has been scarred by what Miranda did to me."

"But we know more now. I think we can protect him," I said.

"I don't think I have the energy for that particular battle again."

"But we have an ace in the hole," I told him.

"What's that?"

"Miranda herself."

12

◇❖◇❖◇❖◇

Weeks passed uneventfully. Liana took a few lessons and was polite but distracted, asking questions that had nothing to do with the horse, like, "Why is that cat staring at me?" or, "Where is the calf whose mother died?"

"Liana, you need to think only of the horse when you're on him. He's aware of your every move, your every thought."

"*Yes, I know*," she said, catching me off guard. "Remember, they talk to me."

"And what is Gringo saying to you right now?"

"Get off me and take me to the barn or I'll dump you!"

"Liana, that's the kindest horse on the guest string!"

"Well, he doesn't like me!" the girl cried. "The only creature in the world who likes me is Hank!"

I noted the word *creature*.

She leaped off the gelding and stomped out of the arena. I followed her, leading Gringo, and called out, "Liana, part of the lesson is taking the saddle off and grooming the horse."

"I don't care. Lessons are over. I'm only coming here to see Hank!" she yelled, just as Hank came out of the main house.

"Liana! My mom's only trying to help you."

"That's what you think! She just wants to keep me away from you!"

"Even if that were true," I said, catching up to her, "this is not the way I'd do it." *Oh, for a lariat!* I thought as she ran into Hank's arms.

"Come on," he said. "I'll brush the horse with you, Liana. But you should apologize to my mother."

"I don't apologize to anyone!" she said, not trying to curb her attitude in the least.

"If you care about me, you will this time," Hank said.

She mumbled something about being sorry, and they took the horse from me. I was proud of Hank, but shaking inside with dread. The girl was headed for a fall. I would not let my son go with her.

Julian's body was healing, but I knew his heart couldn't handle what was happening with Hank. Liana was more subdued with Julian, more respectful, probably because her Hank looked so much like his dad, lean and handsome, alluring and strong. She called him Mr. Rose and deferred to his opinions, even professing to love the horses and ranch life. Julian did not see the lit fuse at the end of the bomb.

Then one morning, Tyrone stood at the front door with a dead puppy in his arms.

"Oh, no, Ty, what went wrong? Couldn't get enough milk?"

"No, ma'am. This was one of the healthiest ones. I believe it was suffocated." He waited awkwardly, clutching the lifeless dog. "Serena, you know how much I love you and Julian …" he said softly.

"Ty, come in the house."

He followed me into the kitchen. Marta and Askay were in the garden. Julian had taken a small group of guests to the Falls, a lovely place we had discovered that summer while scouting a new route to the tent-camp. He wouldn't be back until fairly late in the day. I touched Tyrone's arm and said, "Now, tell me what you know." We had left the puppy outside in a tack box.

"Serena, I've been watching that girl, Hank's friend. At first I thought I was imagining things, being too cautious, but last week I saw her talking to the horses. I couldn't hear what she said, but then she raised her voice. As God is my witness, this is what happened. She said, *Oh you think so? You're going to call me stupid?* And she slapped the horse hard on the face. It can't have been the first time. Some of the horses are getting hard to bridle. When she comes in the barn, the dogs hide. Hank only sees her beauty, her pretty words. He doesn't see her meanness."

I remembered hearing that very word about Miranda.

"I had to say something," Ty finished.

"You did the right thing, Tyrone. You know, Henry Dancing Horse warned me about that girl years ago. I let it go way too long. Next time you see Liana, tell her Hank's mother would like a word with her," I said, holding back the tears. "Don't say anything to Hank or Julian. I'll handle it."

"Okay, Serena, but if I can fix things, you know I will."

"I'll count on that. Now go bury the puppy and move the rest of them into the laundry room here at the ranch house."

"Yes, ma'am."

Of course, the first thing Julian wanted to know was why Paraíso and her brood were in the house. I absolutely could not lie to him. "You'd better sit down … Tyrone thinks Liana killed one of the puppies."

"Oh dear Lord, is that possible?"

"I … I think it is."

"Does Hank know?"

"Not yet."

"He won't believe it," Julian said. "I don't want to believe it."

"Ty's been watching her. He thinks she's … unstable."

"I thought she was warming up to us," Julian said.

"To you, maybe."

Just then, Hank came in looking for Paraíso and the pups. "What's going on? Why can't I find my dog?"

"Hank, she's in the laundry room. Calm down. Ty brought her in after he found one of the puppies dead," I told him.

"Dead? How?"

"We don't know, son," I answered. "It was the big female."

"The one I was going to keep?"

"I think so."

He ran to the back room, calling to his Paraíso.

Julian looked at me with such anguish and said, "Will this never end?"

❖❖❖❖❖

A few days later, Liana walked into the kitchen spoiling for a fight. "Ty sent me over. Said you wanted to see me."

"That's right. Let's go outside."

I made her sit on the swing next to me. I didn't feel like any kind of round pen subtlety was appropriate. It would be the hard truth or nothing at all.

"Liana, what do you know about Hank's puppy, the one who died?"

I was so shocked when she answered, I just stared at her.

"That puppy was going to take Hank away from me, so I had to get rid of it."

I didn't react as she expected, although I felt like hitting her. How could she kill that innocent puppy? But I just said, "Liana, I know something about love that's a train wreck."

"Oh, yeah?"

"Yes. There's a way out of it, but it's not easy."

"Out of what? The love or the train wreck?"

"Maybe both," I said.

"Is this where you tell me what to do?" she asked.

"Oh, you'll have the final choice, but first you need to tell Hank what you've done."

"Or you will?"

"I don't want to. I think the truth must come from you. The truth is a powerful thing. It clears up misunderstandings and suspicions. It opens the way for real love."

"I love Hank. You can't say I don't!"

"If you love him, you'll tell him what happened to his pup. If he loves you, he'll forgive you." That I wasn't so sure of. Julian had not forgiven Miranda for the death of his horses. Did I even want Hank to forgive Liana?

"What makes you think you know so much?"

"Twenty years of marriage and a lot of pain."

"Did you and Mr. Rose hurt each other?"

"No. Let's just say we had to put out a lot of fires to get where we are today."

"I suppose you think *I* might be one of those fires," she said.

"Could be. My son is sort of like dry timber. It wouldn't take much of a blaze to destroy him."

"Are you threatening me?" She narrowed her eyes and leaned toward me.

"Only for your own good, Liana … and mine. I've been through this before. I'm not doing it again. It's not entirely your fault, but I'm going to be blunt. You need to be out of Hank's life. He's too young and, yes, too in love to understand the consequences of a relationship with you. My husband doesn't see it either, because he doesn't want to. I'm twenty years older than the first time I had this conversation with someone, and it sometimes takes everything in me to handle guests and problem horses. Problem humans are no longer on my list."

"You think I'm a problem *now*. Just wait till you try to break me up with Hank," she said in a lethal voice. "Go ahead and tell Hank about the dog yourself. He won't believe you!"

"Maybe not. But the sheriff will," I answered with rising anger.

"You won't call the cops on your son's girlfriend!"

"You're damn right I will," I said. "If you think you can harm my animals or my son without any consequences, you'd better think again, young lady!"

"Oh, you're all bluff. You didn't kick and scream when your precious son lost his virginity!"

"You're right, I should have, but I wasn't sure you were having sex. I'm sure you killed that puppy, and a wrangler has seen you hitting the horses! I'm not going to take any more of this! I'm not sure you can change, Liana, and you may always hate me, but if you love Hank, you'll do what's best for *him*."

"And what's that?" she asked. She shifted uncomfortably on the hard bench of the swing.

"Just leave," I answered. "Leave him alone. You're walking a thin line here. You may think I'm a push-over, but I've got wranglers who could show you consequences the law hasn't even thought of!"

"Hank will never abandon me. He knows how to *forgive*."

"And where do you think he learned that?" I paused to let that sink in, then I said, "Some things are unforgiveable, the torture of animals being one of them."

Liana was walking away. She turned for a moment with pure hatred in her eyes, "I'll get to Hank before you can ever make that phone call!"

She stalked off toward the wash rack where Hank was bathing horses in the hot August day. He gave her a brief hug and tried to go back to his job, but she stripped to a bright blue bikini, and soon they were having a water fight with the hoses. Carson came and retrieved the horse, shaking his head at their antics.

I prayed Hank would see through her lies and went inside. In just a little while, Hank came rushing into the house. "Did you call the sheriff on Liana?"

"No, son. I won't have to do that if she'll stay away from us."

"But why? She told me about the puppy! She said she was just loving it and squeezed too hard. She didn't mean for it to die!"

"She meant for it to die. She's done other things. She's …"

"But, mom, you're the one who always gives people second chances! Who sees the good in people. Why can't you do that with Liana?"

"I don't know, son. There's something wrong with her. How can I give her another chance to hurt one of our animals? Or you?"

"She's not hurting me! I love her."

"Hank, did you know I was spending hours in the round pen gentling many of the horses to be bridled? She's damaged their trust," I told him.

"That's not her! She told me she's seen guests bridling the horses roughly!"

"Now that's just not true!" I said. "We rarely let clients bridle the horses, and you know it. Why would she say such a thing? Who's been in the barn with them lately?"

"She's just trying to help. You're too suspicious."

I felt so helpless at that point I couldn't answer. He seemed ready to cry. "You believe what you want, Hank, but know that I am not blind, and I *will* protect what I love."

The next day, Liana quit her town job, and Hank asked if she could move into one of the guest cabins.

"I have to say no, son. This may be one bronc the round pen can't fix."

"What's that supposed to mean?"

"Think about it. You'll get it," I said trying not to show how appalled I was at the thought of dealing with Liana 24/7.

"Mom," he said intensely, "I need her."

"And I need the souls I love to be safe," I said more calmly than I felt.

"But, mom, you always blame Liana for everything," Hank insisted.

"I don't blame her for everything, just the things she does. You can talk to your father, but I think he'll agree with me. I don't want her on the property."

"Even if that means *I'll* go … to wherever Liana is?"

I hesitated. How could I lose my son to this disaster of a woman? "If you live with her, she'll be committing a crime. Of course, she already has, but I can't prove it. Hank, I'm not going to treat you like a child. I trust you. I don't trust Liana, but if you stay here and be part of this family, these animals, think of their welfare, I'll let her come to see you in the daytime once in a while, maybe stay for dinner *once in a while*."

"Gee, thanks. I'll bet no one ever told you you couldn't be with dad."

"Son, don't you understand? You being with Liana, or rather *her* being with you, is against the law?"

"We're consensual," he said proudly.

"Big word, Hank, that means nothing in court since she's over eighteen and you're not."

"You'd put her in jail?"

"If I have to."

"I guess I have no choice," Hank said. I detected some relief in his voice.

"Not in this, son. When she's here, give her a job, push her a little, and then thank her or blow her a kiss or something. Hey, I've seen a lot of troubled horses change when offered a challenge where they could succeed. But I'll be watching. You can count on that."

So Liana started coming out a couple of times a week. She looked wrathfully at me behind Hank's back, but made a fuss over the puppies and spoke politely to wranglers and guests alike. Julian and I both lay awake at night wondering if we had done the right thing. We let her muck stalls, only when the horses weren't in them. She made a halfhearted attempt to clean tack, but usually Hank or one of the boys had to finish up for her or piece back together bridles with parts in the wrong places. One time, she blasted a stream of cold water on an already shivering horse. Hank yelled at her across the yard, "Turn that off! Liana, what are you doing?"

"He looks filthy. Besides, it's funny to watch him jump off the ground like that," she answered.

"It's not funny," Hank admonished her. He grabbed some towels to rub the horse down and bring some warmth back into his muscles.

She pointed the hose at Hank and drenched him. He lunged for the faucet to shut it off crying, "Liana, cut it out!"

"Can't you take a joke anymore?"

"It's not funny! What's wrong with you?"

"Maybe I need a little more attention around here! You're always off with some cute teenage dude or in the round pen with your mom or running into town and riding home with your dad! I thought I was important to you!"

"You are, but I have other things I have to do. If you can't do chores properly, fine, but let me do mine."

"You didn't have so many chores a few years ago," she accused.

"And maybe I needed to grow up. You should like me better for that."

"Oh, I do, Hank, I do. I love you. I can't stand to be without you. Let's go riding! I can take the little pinto. He doesn't scare me. Come on, Hank, do something with *me*."

Soon, they rode out together toward the Falls which was slowly drying up in the late-season drought, like my patience with the situation. Liana was cautious, but it seemed she was always looking for a way to be in control. She begged Hank to stay in her motel room at night and had a fit when he had appointments to show his puppies. She went on a hunger strike when he traveled with his history teacher and some friends to check out colleges. She left water troughs that she was responsible for cleaning full of moss and mold.

"You can't think of someone else's comfort besides your own for one second!" I shouted at her when I found a detritus-filled trough one hot afternoon.

"The animals don't care about me, why should I care about them?"

"Because life as you know it depends on it," I yelled back.

Ty and Henry Dancing Horse and I had her cornered, but we knew a cornered animal could viciously fight its way out, and we feared that day.

Julian was gone a lot that summer, doing overnights with clients and business in Winnemucca. We all sheltered him from Liana's craziness, praying Hank would hate the divisiveness of her presence and the drain on his own steady nature. They had been friends almost four years, lovers for almost one, but the attraction remained undamaged by Liana's strange behavior.

On a September afternoon, Julian returned early from his Cattlemen's Association meeting. I went out to greet him just as a calico cat darted out from under the porch.

"What happened to Sissy's tail?" he wanted to know. Half of the tail was dead, a skeleton stiff and dry.

"It somehow got caught in a door someone slammed," I said.

"Serena?"

"Oh, it was an accident," I said.

"You mean an accident named Liana."

"I didn't see it, but Hank told me she was mad at him, and the cat got in the way."

"It's just getting to be one too many, isn't it?" he said.

"We have to do something, Julian."

He hugged me, and we went into the ranch house arm in arm.

"Marta," Julian called. She came out of the pantry. "Could you make us some *fever* ice cream?"

"Yes, Mr. Julian. I have all ingredients."

We sat in some easy chairs that had been pulled over by the sketch of Julian bringing in the freezing calf when he was about Hank's age.

"Some innocence, huh?" Julian said.

I kissed his cheek. "I know you don't want to talk about this."

"You want to involve Miranda."

"I think I do, Julian. Hank doesn't see the whole picture. There's only one person who can show him."

"You're right, my dear. Have you seen Miranda lately?"

"A few months ago. She's not doing very well. They think she might have some kind of cancer. They're testing. I've been putting off going back. Can I ask a favor of a dying woman?"

"I think for this you can, but I'm not going with you."

"I know that, Julian. I would never ask you to go. It's very hard for me still. But every time Miranda thanks me for your mom's painting, I know we did the right thing. She'll help us if it's the last thing she does."

A few days later, I drove out to White Pine. Miranda learned most of the story about Hank and Liana. I avoided the death of the puppy for fear of sending her into a tailspin. She listened quietly. The light had gone out of her eyes. Her body was slack and pale. She said, "I know what I can do for you, Serena, and I'm proud to do it. But I don't have a lot of time. My cancer has spread. There's no treatment that I wish to pursue."

She agreed to see Hank for a short talk and then go off her schizophrenia drugs for a week and see Hank again. I didn't know what she'd say, but she was sure he would perceive the gravity of his situation after the two confrontations. She'd have to be shackled for the second visit, but if nothing else, that would scare Hank. She thought maybe Liana should be there for that scene, for her own illumination.

"I'm so tired, Serena. Can you leave me now? I'll think about Julian's son." There was a spark in her eyes the moment she said Julian's name.

"Miranda … I'm sorry."

"Serena, no, I'm resigned. If it wasn't for you, I'd have been dead long ago. You gave me some peace, a way to do the right thing. You kept your promise, and I got to have that special part of Julian, his mother's painting. Don't be sorry for me. Bring me your son. Maybe then Julian," she struggled to finish grabbing the bedpost with some unfathomable pain, "will forgive me."

13

It was Saturday night. Guests, wranglers, Hank, Liana, Julian, and I sat around the big oak table. A cold wind had driven everyone inside early. Askay was putting steaming cucumber/leek soup at each place, saying, "*Karibu, karibu* (you are welcome, you are welcome)." Julian's face was raw from the tears that had fallen as I told him about my visit with Miranda. Everything from the past just flooded his heart. I heard him tell a family from Ojai, California, that the desert air often bothered his eyes. They sympathized, saying that their Santa Ana winds did that to them. I brought him a cold rag to press against his temples, an old trick my grandmother taught me when I cried for hours after leaving my parents' home. Then I looked at Liana.

Her eyes were frantic. Ty hadn't come up from the barn yet, and Hank's girlfriend kept glancing at the door. There was tension in the room that poor Askay tried to soothe away with his African meal. It was so delicious, that blended soup, then a salad of dried cherries and paper-thin slices of sweet onion on garden lettuce, a main dish of grilled lamb in a mango/mint sauce. But I felt guilty enjoying it. Finally Tyrone stuck his head in the door and beckoned to Julian.

Some minutes passed. Julian returned without Ty, and we all continued eating and talking softly. No one missed the gunshot. Julian clutched my hand under the table and said, "Everything's okay, folks." Hank and Liana only had eyes for each other. They didn't know that bullet had pierced their complacency.

After dinner, Ty and Angie played and sang their usual Saturday night routines. The clients danced, and Hank and Liana seemed like Julian and me in those first years, the way they hung on each other with secrets and dreams sealing their fate. Tyrone approached Julian as the time for "Almost Paradise" drew near. Julian said, "Not tonight. I can't let them have that song." The guests started for their cabins, and Julian and I went to our bedroom.

Julian embraced me before the door had even closed and whispered in a dark voice, "She killed Paraíso."

"Oh, God, no, Julian."

"She poisoned her. Ty wanted to end the dog's suffering, so I let him. We agreed to tell Hank she ate a rat that we had baited. Anything else would be too cruel. I can't let my son suffer his whole life because of Liana."

"I have to take him to Miranda," I said.

"I'm going to trust you to do that, Serena. I have no answers. I've been so blind."

"Miranda wants to reveal herself to Hank, on meds and then off meds. Maybe to Liana too. She believes if they see the two Mirandas, it will shock them into getting help. But it's very dangerous for her," I told him.

"Miranda … has cancer?"

"Yes … liver cancer, end stage."

"You care about her," he said with a hint of shock in his voice.

"When have you not cared about a horse in the round pen?" I asked him.

"I started caring after I saw *you* in the round pen, not so much before. The horses were just a part of the business. Oh sure, I had my favorites and spoiled some of them rotten, but care about a bronc like the one in Mom's watercolor? Not a chance."

We heard a cry outside. It must have been Hank discovering his shepherd. If Liana was with him, it should be a knife in her heart. Ty would take the blame for now, saying he was the one who put out poison for the rats. Hank would say something like, *That happens on a ranch, no one's fault,* and take comfort in Liana's arms, which is all she wanted.

Julian and I lay sleepless, shoulders touching, dreading the morning conversation with Hank. "He'll be torn up about his dog. It won't be easy. Hell, I'm torn up about it!" Julian said. "Will the puppies be all right?"

"I'm sure Hank weaned them last week," I said.

"Well, that's a blessing anyway."

We were surprised in the middle of the night to hear Hank open the door to his room, leaving Liana alone in their bed in town. "Grief is a hard partner to own, much less to share," I said.

When we thought Hank was up, at seven, Julian threw on his sweats and met him at the door. "I know about Paraíso, son. I'm so sorry."

"Nothing can bring her back, but thanks, Dad," Hank said, seeming to have no tears left.

"Before you go, your mother and I need to speak to you," Julian told him as I came out of the bedroom.

"Uh oh." He seemed ready for an inquisition.

"You're okay, son," Julian said. "I want to talk about someone I used to know. I'm not going to say much because it's very difficult for me. What your mother and I hope is that you'll let the woman tell you about what happened herself."

"Why?" he asked, still wary.

"Life can throw you a curve sometimes. For you, it came too soon, but we think you're strong enough to withstand it."

"By *curve*, you mean Liana." He was becoming defensive.

"It's more than that, Hank. Just hear us out," Julian pleaded.

I began haltingly. "Hank … fifteen years before I met your father … he married a woman named Miranda."

"Not that crazy Miranda I heard the guys going on about when I was a kid?"

"Yes," I said.

"Why can't *he* talk?" Hank asked, staring at his father.

"Because sometimes the pain eats all the words," I offered.

He softened a little toward Julian, thinking of his own pain, no doubt.

I went on. "Miranda wants to see you. She first asked for that privilege before you were born. Your father said *no*, and that was the end of it. But now things have changed."

"Where is … this Miranda?"

"At White Pine, the mental ward of the women's state prison," I answered.

"I'm not going there!" Hank said.

"There are things she could tell you that we can't," I said.

"What does this have to do with Liana?"

"We want her to go too, but maybe at a different time," I explained.

"She'll never do such a thing!"

"If she truly cares about you, she'll go," I said calmly.

"I just don't see what that crazy woman has to do with Liana and me."

"We're hoping it will become clear to you, son," Julian finally spoke.

"I don't like it," Hank said.

"Sometimes we have to do things we don't like," Julian said.

"Do you *like* this Miranda?" he wanted to know.

"Not really," his dad continued, "but your mother has quite literally saved her life, so Miranda feels in her debt. She thinks she can save you some heartache, at least."

"My heart is just fine," Hank said.

"There's a thin line between fine and devastated. Trust me," his father said.

"I'll go because I'm curious. That's the only reason. And it better be worth it."

"You'll decide the worth of it for yourself," I said. "Now go do your chores. And Hank, losing your dog, that shouldn't have happened. I'll never forget her or why she died."

"Thanks, Mom. I know you guys loved her too."

"What did Liana say?" Julian dared to ask.

"We kind of had a fight about it. She said, 'Too bad about your dog, but now we'll have more time for us.' God, sometimes she says the oddest things. I guess they can't be any worse than what that *Miranda* might say."

"One thing you should know, Hank," I added. "Miranda is dying. I believe she will tell you the truth."

"Well, either I'll believe her or I won't. I guess we'll see," he said, and he was out the door.

Julian sat down at the kitchen table and called to Marta. She rushed over, and he put his hand on her shoulder. "Marta, make me a *fever cocktail* and put everything Askay has in it!"

"Make that two, Marta," I said, and we all smiled a smile of hope.

14

◇◇◇◇◇◇

Hank buried Paraíso by her pup, and I thought, *Two birds with one stone*. Liana stood behind him, her face blank. She got impatient and begged him, "Hank, let's go to Winnemucca for a few days. I'm really bored with this place. We need to have some fun."

He answered right back, "I can't. I'm doing something with my mom in a couple of days."

Liana glared at me, and I thought, *Jesus, I'd better not see her near the kitchen!*

"Where are you two going?" she asked with a jealous expression.

"To White Pine Women's Prison."

She blanched and clapped her hand to her mouth, then recovered enough to ask, "Why on earth?"

"To meet my father's first wife."

Oh Lord, Hank, when you tell the truth, you really go for it, I thought, inwardly amazed.

"Instead of going to Winnemucca with me?" she whined.

"Yep."

"Can I go with you?" she asked, a little more submissive.

Hank looked at me. He couldn't know what a godsend that request was.

I said, "As a matter of fact, Miranda wants to talk to you too, but a week later."

"I may be going back to work by then," she said, hedging her bets.

"Well, that's up to you," I said casually. "I don't think it will change anything for Hank, but you might learn something. The woman had a tough life and wants to show you young people how to avoid what she's suffered." *And what suffering she has caused*, I added silently.

It was a long two days. Miranda's doctor called and said he didn't like the idea of his patient going off her meds for a week, especially in her fragile condition. "She's determined to do it, so let's get it over with as soon as possible," he said.

"We're coming tomorrow," I told him.

I didn't think it was possible that I would ever trust Miranda completely, but I knew she would remind herself that Hank was the grandson of the woman whose painting had given her a second chance, an anchor.

We arrived at the appointed time and went together to Miranda's room. Hank wouldn't go without me. When we entered, we saw that Miranda was in handcuffs and shackles. She apologized, explaining that this was the policy when one had two visitors. "I guess they think the extra person might be an accomplice planning to break the prisoner out." She laughed weakly at the irony.

Hank hung back by the door, looking scared.

"It's all right, young man. I deserve your scorn. I'm not a nice person."

Hank didn't move, so she went on. "I know this is hard for you. I don't know how much your parents have told you."

"They said you were my dad's first wife," Hank said, moving a little closer to the chained-up woman.

"May I call you Hank?"

He nodded. Then she looked at me. "I know you don't want to hear all this again, Serena. I have to tell him everything."

"It's all right, Miranda."

She paused, as if searching for the breath to speak, and then said, "Hank, I truly loved your father for several months more than thirty-five years ago. But I was ill, and nobody knew how to help me. Right now, I'm on pretty strong drugs, and I seem fairly normal, right?"

"Yeah," Hank said, sitting down in a chair closer to Miranda than to me.

Her hair was freshly washed, and she had on a new dress, not the orange jumpsuit. The blush on her face could have been from fever or makeup, but it softened her appearance.

Hank said, "I'm sorry they locked you like that because I wouldn't come in without my mom."

"That's very generous of you, Hank, but you're probably going to hate me before I'm through."

"What did you do?"

"I killed two of your father's best horses."

"Oh my God," Hank said with a fist to his mouth.

"I set fire to them inside his horse trailer."

"But why? Why would you do such a thing?"

"Because I thought he loved them more than he loved me. Because I thought with his horses gone, he would have more time for me, for us."

Hank stared at her as if he'd seen a ghost, heard those words before.

"What was your illness?" he asked, beginning to pale.

"Schizophrenia," she answered. "Voices urged me to kill those animals, told me they were taking my place with your father."

Hank fought his emotions valiantly, but tears rolled down his face. He glanced out the small window and then noticed the painting on the wall.

"Your grandmother painted that. Helen Rose. It saved my life. Go look closely, Hank."

My son went to look at the picture. He touched the name *Helen Rose*, as Miranda and I had done so many times.

"It's beautiful," he said.

"And do you know what the most beautiful thing is, Hank? The arm that's reaching for the scared colt is Helen's arm."

"She painted herself in the picture?" he asked.

"Yes, Hank. Little did she know what that gesture might mean, or maybe she did. All these years, I've felt your grandmother's arm reaching out to me in my pain and confusion, in my dark mind, and now in my cancer-ridden body. I'm the untamed horse. I'm the frightened colt. The men were ready to break me, to shatter my spirit, but Julian's mother saw a different way. Your mother, Serena, saw a different way."

"What does this have to do with me?"

"Well, no one wants to tell you this, but I'm dying and have nothing to lose. You can hate me for what I did to your father, but it won't keep me from protecting you from the same violence. Come sit down."

Hank moved back to the chair. Miranda put her cuffed hands on Julian's son. "Have you lost any animals lately?" she asked.

"Yes ... how did you know? Did my mom tell you?"

"Not exactly ... She told me about Liana. I figured out the rest. Your girlfriend killed those animals. She needs help. She needs medication, and you need to get as far away from her as you can."

"Mom?"

"It's true, Hank," I said.

"I know it's true," Miranda said, "because it's what I did to keep Julian for myself. Liana is ill. I'm going to stop my meds and let you both see me next week. You'll understand what this disease can do. You'll get help or you'll run, but I'll tell you this. Your parents' hearts are breaking for you. They know the terror of facing someone like me."

Hank had his head in his hands, a thing I had seen his father do more than once. "Ty wouldn't tell me what really happened to the puppy. Liana told me she accidently hugged it too hard, that I could have a lot more puppies, why did that one matter so much? *Because I was going to keep that one*, I said. Liana said, *Now you can keep me*."

"You knew there was something wrong with her, didn't you?" Miranda said.

"Yeah."

"Just like your father knew there was something wrong with me. But he didn't do anything about it till it was too late. He spent fifteen years waiting for me to get well. And then I almost killed him, for a second time actually, out on the desert twenty years ago."

"What happened?" Hank asked.

"Your mother threw a rope on me and spoiled my aim," she said, conjuring up that vision of my hand on the end of the lariat below Towering Peak.

"Miranda?" Hank brought her back into the room. "What would you say to Liana?"

"I don't know. I'm going off my meds so you can see the real me. I'm hoping it will scare her into getting some help and you into getting away from her."

"You don't have to do that," Hank said. "She might not come, and you'll have suffered for nothing."

"If Liana doesn't understand what's going to happen to her, she'll never leave you alone. You'll live in her shadow, never knowing what she might do to the things you love."

"How can I explain *you* to her? There aren't any words," Hank said.

"But there's a picture." She rose unsteadily and shuffled over to the wall where Helen's watercolor had hung all these years.

"Come ... and take this painting, Hank. It's yours now—your grandmother's brush strokes, your grandmother's hand with the gift of love for the colt. I don't need it where I'm going. It's in my heart anyway."

She sank to the bed. At that moment, there was a knock on the door. An official entered, saying, "Three is against the rules," as Julian came in behind him.

"I couldn't let you do it without me," he said.

"Dad! Look what Miranda gave me!" He held the painting up proudly.

Julian melted at the sight of Helen's watercolor.

Miranda looked up at the face she had seen only once in two decades. "Julian," she whispered.

"Miranda, I'm going to get those chains off! This is an outrage." And he stepped outside. We could hear him say firmly, "This woman is ill. There's no need for the cuffs. She's doing a great thing for us. I put her here. I demand you remove those shackles!"

"Yes, sir, Mr. Rose. We didn't realize you were coming."

He came back in the room and went toward his ex-wife.

"I don't deserve such kindness from you," Miranda said.

"Miranda, I forgive you," Julian said and sat down on the narrow bed next to her. Her eyes sparkled briefly. He took her hands. She made a little gasp and hooked her fingers through his.

"You have a beautiful son, you and Serena. Have you had a good life, Julian?"

"Yes, Miranda, the best."

"Thank you for letting Serena visit me. She brought me gifts, you know. My butter mints, my scarves. Look, I have one on now." She touched a faded paisley print that I had wrapped around her shoulders over ten years ago. "And for your forgiveness, I'm deeply grateful," she said, barely able to say the words.

"I should have done more for you, Miranda," Julian said.

"No … you let me save your son. That is worth the meaning of my whole life. And now I must let you go. My hands are free, my feet are free, my heart is free … because of you."

Hank leaned down and kissed her, and I wiped a tear from her cheek.

"Serena," she said, "I've loved you since you first swung that rope over my head and said, *Look me in the eyes, I'm going to help you.* Remember that, dear one. I think this is good-bye."

"Miranda … God be with you," I said, and I really meant it.

We left White Pine, Hank clutching the painting with newfound awareness of the strangeness of our journey, the knowledge of what he must do for himself, for Liana, and for us. He wanted to ride with his dad, so I got in my truck alone. Then I suddenly rushed back to the facility and asked to see Miranda briefly. They led me to her room where she was lying down, breathing uneasily.

"Oh, Serena, what is it?"

"Miranda, I want to know where you would like to be laid to rest."

"Really?"

"Yes. You say, and I'll do it," I promised.

"At the foot of Towering Peak," she said, clear as a bell.

She closed her eyes, and that was the last time I saw her. On the way out, I explained that Julian and I would handle the final arrangements, and then I headed back to the ranch with the Nevada sun making its dramatic departure from the desert through superb violets and ambers, black sketches of storm banking on the horizon, light transforming the colors minute by minute, my own soul transformed by the power of forgiveness and love.

15

◇◇◇◇◇◇

That night, Hank carried Helen's picture over to one of the cabins where we said they could stay just this once. We had no idea what he would say, barely sixteen and thrown into the turbulence of mental illness and wrenching good-byes. He came back about midnight. We were still in the kitchen, sharing a dish of *fever* ice cream.

"She admitted everything. She said she needs help." He paused. "She said she doesn't want to lose me, but when I told her I couldn't watch her fall like Miranda into such a terrible and dangerous place, she started freaking out, asking what was so *terrible*, what was so damn awful. I told her Miranda was going to show us next week after she'd been off her meds. Liana said she didn't want to see that. I said if she didn't come with me, to really understand the problem, that I didn't have the strength or the heart for our relationship. She cried. Well, she more than cried. She said if I turned my back on her, there would be a price to pay. I ... left the painting over there. She said it comforted her."

"You did what you had to do, son," Julian said. "Are you okay?"

"I couldn't forgive her for killing my dogs. I couldn't be you, Dad," he said.

"It took me many years to get to that place," Julian admitted. "Everything's in Liana's hands now."

And it couldn't have been truer. In the morning, she was gone, with one of Paraíso's pups and Helen's painting. She left no note or sign that she had ever loved Robert Henry Askay Rose.

Hank started running again, and Julian and I closed down the ranch for winter. We spent a few days at the canyon house, finding in each other's arms peace and *almost* paradise. The loss of Helen's watercolor weighed on Julian, but we thought if it could lead Liana to a safer place, it would be okay.

Early snow drove us down onto the flats. The ranch was quiet, some cowboys gone till next season, others patching up corrals and fences before the gathering storms. Marta and Askay were in their eighties now, and we asked if they wanted to retire. They already had the answer they hoped we liked. Marta had a grandniece graduating from Cal Poly who could come next summer and take over Marta's duties. Askay had saved enough money for a plane ticket and a work visa for his grandson to emigrate from Tanzania. Our two faithful friends would remain at the ranch. It was their home.

On a bitter November day, Julian and I buried Miranda in the lonely patch of sand beneath Towering Peak where she had first stood in the round pen with wild eyes and unrepentant heart. I was fifty-one and Julian sixty-two, but in the dim winter light at the end of the day, we could have been our younger selves, weary of the threat of Miranda, filled only with love for each other and the paradise we owned.

Now a piece of us dropped into the earth with Miranda, moved swiftly across the Nevada tracks with Hank's long legs, and drifted somewhere with Helen's painting on the trajectory of Liana's pain. The wind blew its steady breath against us as we stood arm in arm beside the grave. We didn't speak, cleansed of bitter and reprieving words alike, till in the seasons to come, only words of love between us remained.

16

On my sixtieth birthday, Julian laid a package on the table in front of me with a secret smile. I carefully folded back the brown paper and gazed down at the painting, Helen's arm reaching through the round pen, the colors only slightly faded, a scratch in the canvas here and there.

"Oh, Julian, oh, dear Lord, how …"

"I found it at an art auction in Winnemucca last month! I could hardly keep it from you!"

I looked at the haunting image. "Where have you been?" I asked, holding it up to the light.

"On its own journey, with or without Liana," Julian answered.

"Let's hang it in the barn," I said, "for our last season. It could still save a horse or two."

"You can't take the round pen out of the cowgirl," he teased.

We walked to the barn, the painting between us, our paradise spread out across the buttes and canyons and clean, white sand, ending at the oak fences that were acres distant. But the paradise in our hearts, the one we had forged together—riding and dancing, making love and raising a child—that paradise had no end.

Read the first chapter of the forthcoming sequel to
Almost Paradise, Dancing in the Red Snow.

DANCING IN THE RED SNOW

Elizabeth Cain

1

⬦⬦⬦⬦⬦

Henry Four Names walked with anguished steps out across the Nevada landscape, tears and rain lashing his cheeks and half blinding him. He was leading his horse now. The others had spread out, searching, calling his mother's and father's name. Thunder obliterated the sound, driving it into the ravaged ground. Little rivulets had formed in the dry ravines. The horses stumbled on the slick sandstone hills, weary of this ceaseless wandering and circling.

Billy galloped up on his burgundy colt, the offspring of a coveted line from his roan mare. The horse was shaky on his young legs. The wrangler called to Henry, "Hank! What's the last thing they said? Anything. Anything you remember!"

"Just, *We're going to take a short ride, son. Should be back before the storm rolls in.* That's all."

Hank swallowed his panic and tried to reason out what might have happened. They could have gone in any direction. The ranch covered twenty thousand acres. He thought of the day his father had come home with the deed for the ten-thousand-acre tract to the north. He was like a kid in a candy shop, flashing his generous smile and lifting his mother off her feet. *We're not done yet!* he'd cried.

His folks had planned for that season to be their last. They were worn out giving dudes a taste of ranch life, teaching guests to *reward the slightest change* in their assigned horses in the round pen, and running a huge herd of Brahmans. But on a summer day under a truly azure sky, they rode off their property after a group of cows that had gone through the north boundary with their calves, leaving the oak posts and rails broken and scattered in a perpetually damp draw that had weakened the structure of the fence.

They trotted onto part-government land, part-old-Spanish rancho run by proxy by descendants of the Molina family in Florida. It was exquisite country. The elevation rose to almost ten thousand feet through forests of Washoe pine and ponderosa. Several lakes were scattered among the towering trees, granite outcrops, and fields of desert sunflowers, primrose, purple mountain sage, too many varieties of penstemon to count, rock fringe along the trail, and rein orchids hovering around the marshy edges.

Julian and Serena had found the cows and calves by one of these clear ponds and watched a golden eagle land on an old snag reaching up out of the sparkling water. The grasses were unblemished by weeds and included healthy grains, timothy and wild oats that nothing had grazed but elk and mule deer. "Another paradise," Julian had said to Serena. "I feel called to its life, its beauty. How can we quit before we've discovered its secrets?"

"I'm up for whatever you are. This looks like heaven to me," she had told her husband.

And so, Rancho del Cielo Azul had stayed open five more seasons. They called the new territory *Heaven's Door*.

Hank mounted and turned toward the jewel of the north, beckoning several of the wranglers closest to him to follow. "They must've gone this way!" he shouted. In a mile, they crossed a dry plateau where little rain had fallen, and there in a sandy stretch were the hoof prints of Julian and Serena's horses, the distinctive W of the special shoes on his father's gelding mixed with the fainter mark of his mom's unshod mare.

Hank began calling their names again. The boys were tired, their horses lagging now on the steeper climbs into *Heaven's Door*. The gals had stayed behind with Susan. His heart lurched. His wife was close to delivering their first child. She had been so uncomfortable this last week that he had been afraid to leave her alone. He felt ripped into two pieces, one part of him reaching out toward the fate of his parents, the other pulled back to his beautiful Susan Sun, suffering who-knows-what back at the ranch house. In that moment he did not believe in God, but was praying just the same for everyone to be safe.

Pete had to turn back. His horse was done. Billy was using the end of his lariat now to keep his colt going. His face was grim and determined. Hank thought of the stories his dad had told him about Billy, how the boy's folks had abandoned him at the ranch when he was eleven, and Julian had told the boy, "Just stay. Your home is here now." Billy was fifty-three and had never married. He had given his life to Julian and Serena's dream, and now he streaked back and forth like a madman, studying the confusing signs of his patrons' horses on the unforgiving earth.

Tyrone, a few hundred yards ahead, had been the foreman as long as Hank could remember. He'd led Hank as a child out onto the desert on Sparkle, his first pony, showed him how to clean the hooves and tie an emergency hitch to a rail. Ty was about sixty and limped some with arthritis in his hip after hours in the saddle.

And farther ahead, riding across the old north boundary, was Henry Dancing Horse, his mom's protégé and Hank's first Native American friend, who had taken his hand when Hank was six years old and never let go, calling him Henry Four Names from the beginning and teaching him the sacred Indian way. He reached down in his pocket and touched the Apache Tear, a smooth chunk of black obsidian he had carried with him for twenty-five years. Now it felt as hard and lifeless as his hope.

Hank could hardly think. It had been a few hours since Julian and Serena's horses had come back to the ranch, wild-eyed and stunned. His mom's saddle had a ragged black slash on the left fender, and her mare was favoring that side. His father's horse collapsed in the barnyard and was still not up, as far as Hank knew. But the gelding was alive when everyone raced out from the ranch to find Julian and Serena.

The minutes seemed like hours, the desperation multiplying beyond consolation in the minds of the searchers, darkening as the sky darkened to obliterate the trail. Finally, a few wranglers had halted their mounts and were looking down into a deep arroyo on the edge of the first fringe of pines stalking up a long ridge into the heart of *Heaven's Door*. James held three or four horses while the riders scrambled down into the ravine and then shouted up to everyone, "We found them!"

Robert Henry approached the scene on the rain-soaked desert, fear rising in him like the magma of some pent-up volcano. *Oh, God, please, please let them be okay,* he prayed silently. But it was not to be. Tyrone grabbed his shoulders and tried to keep him from the sight in the gorge. Hank pushed him away, clambered down the muddy bank, and went helplessly to his knees where his mother and father lay. They had done the right thing, curled up together in the ditch, holding on, as they always had, to their incandescent love, which Hank imagined in that moment must have flamed up to meet the lightning in its path to earth.

Julian had one arm around Serena, his other arm flung at an odd angle and black as the sky above them. Hank's mother was so beautiful at sixty-five, so strikingly real in the shadows of *Heaven's Door*, he couldn't understand that she would never look at him with her azure eyes and say, "Hank, my boy, I'll be all right." She didn't look as hurt as Julian, just still, still and silent as new rain pelted their bodies and the smell of wet burn filled the air.

And then, there was nothing Hank could do. Billy lifted him from the cruel death, struggling with his own emotions, and said, "I'm here for you," as Julian must have said to him so many years ago. The storm moved east as they trotted back to the ranch, and some ironic blue broke through the lightning-laced clouds. A couple of the guys offered to ride ahead and hitch up the camp wagon to retrieve the bodies. But as they tightened their horses' girths and prepared themselves to bear Julian and Serena out of the drainage, Hank said, with more strength in his voice than he felt, "Don't separate them."

CPSIA information can be obtained at www.ICGtesting.com
Printed in the USA
BVOW08*1417110813

328126BV00001B/2/P